GOING BIG OR SMALL

David Canford

COPYRIGHT © 2018 DAVID CANFORD

9.24

All rights reserved. No part of this publication may be reproduced, distributed, or transmitted in any form or by any means, or stored in a database or retrieval system, without the prior written permission of the author.

This novel is a work of fiction and a product of the author's imagination. Any resemblance to anyone living or dead (save for named historical figures) or any entity or legal person is purely coincidental and unintended.

Cover design by Mary Ann Dujardin

CHAPTER 1

"Your father's becoming a gypsy."
Frank's ex-wife, Gayle, let out a screech reminiscent of a mating fox. A sort of high pitched screaming, which was her inimitable way of laughing.
"A nomad," Frank corrected her.
"A hippie more like. And over twenty years too late. You've missed the summer of love. And as for taking your clothes off, it doesn't bear thinking about."
"I won't be doing that."
"Oh, but they all do over there. On the beach in St Tropez this summer, it wasn't just the girls without bikinis. Men with their little button mushrooms were everywhere. It stopped me from dozing off, I can tell you."
Gayle bent over forwards and then popped back up like a spring as she laughed at the memory.
"You have to hand it to the French, they've got a lot of self-confidence. Strutting around, proud as peacocks in their birthday suits. Morris left the beach faster than a rat up a drain pipe when I asked

him if he was going to join them. After all, why not I said. I'd gone topless."

Frank winced at the images she'd created in his mind.

"Why dad?" sighed Dawn, their daughter while she tried to get her own daughter, Sinead, to stop bawling at the top of her lungs by gently swinging her from side to side in her arms.

"It's something different. I've always fancied travelling around Europe but I couldn't ever afford it. I've got my pension coming in now, and that'll be enough to live on in a camper van and pay the bills back home for a few weeks. A friend of mine knows someone who's selling his. It's only a small one apparently, but it'll be plenty big enough for me."

Gayle's dyed auburn hair was still moving from tossing her head back and forwards while she'd laughed. Her left eyebrow remained much higher than the right one. Probably the effect of too much plastic surgery, thought Frank. It was strange how she'd had a complete makeover when she met Morris. You spend your life thinking you know someone so well only to discover that you never really did.

"He's never been anywhere more foreign than a Chinese restaurant, and he didn't even like that."

Gayle was almost crying with laughter by now.

"Life is short," said Frank.

"Yours will be when you're driving on the wrong side of the road. I take it you do know that? They all drive on the other side. It's very confusing. Morris had a couple of near misses coming back from France. Didn't you, Morris?"

Morris didn't answer.

"Who's going to look after Sinead and Oliver on Tuesdays and Thursdays?" interjected Dawn.

"Maybe your mum-"

"No, Monday is the only day I can manage, you know that. Morris needs me around the rest of the week to help entertain his clients, don't you dear?"

"Don't you think you're being a bit selfish, dad?" said Dawn.

"No, not really. If I wait until your kids are old enough to be left, I'll be too old to go."

"Well, thanks for making the christening so memorable."

Dawn stormed out into the garden to mingle with other guests.

"What about the lingo?" asked Morris. "Parlez-vous Francais? Sprechen Sie Deutsch?"

"Oh, you're so talented, Morris. I love it when you speak Spanish. It makes my toes curl."

Gayle kissed his cheek, which was tanned orange from lying on a sunbed at the local salon.

"I'll manage," said Frank. "English is universal these days."

"Don't you believe it. The French are happy to let you struggle, even if they speak English, aren't they, Morris? I feel like I've been struck dumb when I'm over there."

Morris tilted his head to one side and raised his

eyebrows ever so slightly, as though wishing it wasn't only in France Gayle was forced to keep quiet.

"Well, I better be going. Got a lot to do. Goodbye, Abigail and Morris."

Frank knew she didn't like being called by her full name, but he'd had enough of her today. He was relieved to get away. He didn't enjoy family gatherings much. The problem was Frank didn't seem to enjoy anything these days.

His life was in a rut. Recently retired and with too much time on his hands, the remainder of his life stretched out in front of him like the wet Sundays of his childhood when there was nothing to do. A roast lunch with his mum and dad over at his grandparents, and having to sit quietly afterwards while they all slept in the armchairs with their mouths open. They'd wake up when one of them snorted on a snore and look around in surprise for a moment before their heads flopped either backwards or forwards as they resumed their nap. It was true Frank hadn't been abroad, but then they'd never had enough money while the kids were growing up to do that. Maybe that's what Gayle had found so appealing about Morris. He had been able to give her excitement, jetting off several times a year to adult toy exhibitions all over the globe. That's what his company sold, and very successfully too it would seem from their big house next to the golf course with expensive sports cars on the driveway behind their remotely

GOING BIG OR SMALL?

controlled gates painted in gold.

It reminded Frank of South Fork from the TV series 'Dallas'. Gayle always said she wished she could live like Sue Ellen when they used to watch the show and now she did.

Frank drove back to his two up, two down in a street of identical terraced houses. He'd lived there ever since marrying Gayle nearly forty years ago. You walked in straight off the pavement. There was no garden out front, no separation from the street outside.

It had seemed like a palace to them when they'd moved in. Now the area had gone downhill. The house on one side of his was boarded up, unoccupied except for the drug addicts who went in there to inject themselves. He'd stepped in their vomit more than once coming out of his front door.

The man with the camper van for sale would be popping round this evening. A chap down at the pub had arranged it, he'd said it was a friend of a neighbour of his wanting to sell.

Frank heard it before he saw it. A throaty sound like one of those East European cars.

Not only did it sound old fashioned, it also looked it. Like a poor man's Volkswagen camper van, though it didn't have such smooth lines. It started and ended abruptly. The front and rear lights protruded, like a design afterthought. Still, from the front it was quite endearing, a sort of 'Thomas the Tank Engine' appeal, the round lights giving it a cartoonish appearance. As did its radiator grille, which was a large oblong as if the vehicle was permanently happy with a wide-open smiling mouth.

Frank who had lifted the net curtain at the front window to look, let it drop and went outside.

"Bugger!" he said as the front door closed behind him. He'd failed to leave it on the latch and had forgotten to bring his key.

"Hello, I'm Erika."

Frank did a double take. He wasn't expecting to meet a woman, even less one who looked like she was in Abba with her long blonde hair and knee-high boots.

CHAPTER 2

"Frank Braithwaite."
"What do you think, Frank?"
"It's pink."
"Yes, probably not your colour. I had it resprayed a couple of years ago."
"What is it? I've never seen one like it before."
"It's a Barkas. They're manufactured in East Germany."
"Oh."
Frank knew of Russian Ladas and Moscovitches and East German Wartburgs. He'd even seen a few on the roads. People bought them if they couldn't afford a car made in the West. They were dirt cheap by comparison. But he'd never heard of the Barkas.
"Did you want to look inside?"
"May as well. Oh, it's left-hand drive," said Frank as he climbed in.
"Yes, handy if you're thinking of travelling around Europe like Bob told me."
"Good point, I hadn't thought of that."
Inside, the vehicle had two front seats. Behind on one side were a small gas hob, a sink and a cupboard. At the back was a sofa which Erika

proceeded to demonstrate converted into a double bed by pulling it out so that it was flush against the kitchen area. For two stick insects perhaps, thought Frank. It wasn't much wider than a single bed. But then it would only be him sleeping in it so that didn't matter.

"Would you like to go for a drive?"

"All right, why not."

As they set off, Frank noticed Mrs Moore from next door quickly pulling her head back behind her curtain. There wasn't much that happened on this street she didn't know about.

The ride wasn't smooth but it was adequate. Frank felt a buzz of excitement at the thought this vehicle could be his. His very own home on wheels. He didn't often feel a buzz. In fact, Frank couldn't remember the last time he'd felt one.

When they got back, he walked around the vehicle, stroking his chin and frowning, pretending he was knowledgeable about cars which he wasn't.

"How old is it?"

"I'm not sure. I brought it over from Sweden after buying it there five or six years ago."

Frank smiled. Just like Abba, she was Swedish. Not that he'd been a big fan of the group. Dawn was though, playing their records at full volume when she was a teenager, and Gayle had been fond of singing their songs out loud around the house. The group was too modern for him. Still, their music helped fill their long empty silences once the children moved out.

GOING BIG OR SMALL?

Gayle's favourite was "Knowing me, Knowing you". Frank should have got a hint from the lyrics:
"Knowing me, knowing you (ah-ha)
There is nothing we can do
"Knowing me, knowing you (ah-ha)
We just have to face it, this time we're through."
"Why are you selling it?" asked Frank.
"I'm moving to Australia. I'll miss her, she's been good to me."
"She?"
"Yes, Brunhild. One of the Valkyries."
"Oh, right. I'm not familiar with their songs. Not really into pop music myself."
Erika laughed.
"No, not a pop group. The Valkyries were Norse goddesses. Brunhild was a mighty warrior. Anyway, you can't have a pink van with a man's name, can you."
"No, I suppose not. How much do you want for it - I mean her?"
"A thousand."
"A thousand pounds?"
"It's a good price. I'm assuming you know what the more popular camper vans cost. And you've got to admit, it's well fitted out."
"Eight hundred."
"Nine."
"Agreed. I'll get the cash tomorrow."
"Great. I'll be round at five if that's okay."
Frank nodded. He watched Erika and Brunhild leave. With an uncharacteristic bounce in his step,

he headed for his door until he recalled he was locked out.

"Anything the matter, Frank?"

Mrs Moore stood at her front door with her arms folded across her apron, a mischievous twinkle in her eye.

"I locked myself out."

"Yes, I happened to notice that."

"You wouldn't have a ladder, would you? The bathroom window upstairs at the back is open."

"I think so. Bert used to keep one in the shed. Come and have a cup of tea first, then we'll go look."

Inwardly, Frank grimaced. She always asked so many questions but he couldn't refuse.

"Sit yourself down while I put the kettle on."

A few minutes later she returned, carrying a tray with two cups of tea and some cakes.

"Rock buns," she proudly announced, offering him a plate.

Frank remembered having one at hers before. They had lived up to their name.

"I won't thanks. It'll put me off my dinner."

And I don't want to break a tooth, but he didn't say that part out loud.

"That was a strange car you were looking at. Not that I was being nosey you understand, just passing the window."

"It's a camper van."

"I've always fancied a caravan myself. A home from home. But with Bert gone, bless his soul, that won't happen now. Are you thinking of touring the country?"

"Europe."

"Europe? Well, you do surprise me. I never had you down as the adventurous type."

Frank didn't reply. He drank some tea, burning his mouth in the process because he didn't want to wait for it to cool down or Dorothy Moore would be offering to come along.

"Do you mind if we get the ladder? I left something cooking in the oven," he lied.

Mrs Moore watched while he climbed up it and into the window at the back of his house.

"I'll bring it back in a little while and put it in your shed. Thanks for all your help," he shouted down.

That night, Frank couldn't sleep. Sixty-five years he'd lived in this town, never going far. His life had been very pedestrian, leaving school at sixteen and working in the same factory until retiring earlier this year. He had a daughter, a son who he never saw these days, and a wife until she'd left him for Morris.

It was when he retired earlier in the year that he had experienced that "oh shit" moment. His life was moving into the last act. A slow decline which would accelerate before too long. If he didn't do something exciting now he never would. This was his last chance.

He applied for a passport, his very first. It was impressive. Gold lettering and the Queen's coat of arms. Something about Her Britannic Majesty requiring all those who it concerned to allow the bearer to pass freely.

And tomorrow he was getting his camper van. No excuses not to go travelling now. Freedom. The open road. A latter-day James Dean. The prospect frightened him, yet it also made him feel alive. And that, like getting a buzz out of life, was something which he had forgotten what it was like to feel.

The first thing would be to get the van resprayed. Frank didn't want to spend the next few weeks looking like he was exiting a flamingo each time he got out of it.

Erika cried when she said goodbye to Brunhild. She hugged it by putting one arm across the front window and the other down the side. Being British, Frank looked away. Emotions were something to keep repressed, the stiff upper lip and all that.

When she'd finished, he offered her a lift in the old Toyota he owned but she said she preferred to walk.

Arthur Bates from down the road laughed as he passed by.

"Bloody hell, Frank. That's a bit girlie."

"I'm going to get it painted."

"Make sure you do or they'll be talking about you down at the Queen Mary."

"What on earth did you buy a Commie car for?" Fred challenged Frank down at the pub that evening.

"It was a good price."

"So's any bunch of crap. And why are you going

to Europe anyway? What have they got that we haven't?"

"I don't know. That's what I'll find out."

And I won't have to listen to you and your opinions, thought Frank.

"I was there in the war. Awful place," said Fred.

"It's probably changed. That was over forty years ago."

Frank wondered if he'd miss the other men he propped up the bar with every evening between six and seven, putting the world to rights with a pint of beer and a packet of pork scratchings. It was an unloved place, its walls stained yellow from years of a fog of nicotine floating around those who gathered there, but it was a place where people knew his name.

CHAPTER 3

Frank finished packing and was about to leave to catch a night ferry to Rotterdam when there was a knock at the door. He muttered crossly, he didn't want any visitors.
"Dawn. What are you doing here?"
"I brought you something. I thought maybe I was a bit grumpy the other day."
"Come in."
She gave him a package wrapped in silver paper.
"What is it?"
"Open it and you'll find out."
"A tape recorder?"
"No, you daft apeth. It's a Walkman. A Sony Walkman. You put your cassettes in it and put the headphones on. I thought you could listen to that awful music of yours."
"Ah, thanks love."
"Well, I must be off. Stay safe now."
"I will. I'm only going for a few weeks. I'll be back before you know it."
When she'd gone, Frank had another of those 'why the hell am I doing this' moments. He was already

nervous about leaving his safe and boring world. He could just stay. Go on as before. Watch TV every night and have hot cocoa before bed.

And get to the end of his life having done very little at all. No, nothing ventured, nothing gained. For once, Frank was determined.

A few minutes later, there was another knock. Gayle's mascara was smudged as if she'd been crying.

"Can I come in?"

"I suppose so. I'm just about to-"

"I've left Morris."

Gayle had already pushed past him and sat herself down on the bright red leather sofa which she'd insisted they buy a few years back.

"Whatever for?" asked Frank.

"I came home early from the hairdressers as they'd mixed up my appointment and caught him shagging some twenty-something on our leopard skin rug no less. It was horrible, like Quasimodo had crash-landed face down but without any clothes on. I used to love that rug. I won't ever be able to look at it again in the same way. That poor leopard has a good excuse now for looking so startled."

"Oh dear."

"Oh dear? Is that all you've got to say?"

"Well, it's not really any of my business."

"Do you mind if I stay here tonight in the spare bedroom? I can't impose myself on Dawn, and when I tried to check in at the Priory Hotel, I found out that the sneaky bastard has already taken me off his credit cards. Tomorrow, I'll be straight down at the lawyers. He's not going to know what's hit him. Make me a cup of tea, can you? And bring the biscuit tin back with you. I've been traumatised."

"Actually, I'm just leaving."

"You're not still planning to drive around the Continent, are you? It's about time you acted your age. You're a pensioner now. We all think you've gone bonkers."

Frank didn't say anything as Gayle got up, tutted with annoyance and left, although he did shout be careful when she sped off in her Jaguar sports car just missing his van. Not that she would have heard with the roar her car made as it accelerated away.

Locking the front door and putting his suitcase into the van, Frank noticed Dorothy Moore walking towards him holding a tin with a picture of a snowman on the lid.

"I made you one of my fruitcakes. Something to keep you going if you don't like the food over there. I've heard they'll eat anything. Horse meat, even."

"Thank you very much. I'll look forward to eating it."

"A cup of tea before you go?"

"No thanks, I'm already late."

With a hesitant wave, Frank climbed in and drove off down the familiar streets, passing his old school and the factory where he had worked for nearly fifty years. All the old certainties, uninspiring but unthreatening.

When he reached the motorway, Frank discovered Brunhild's top speed was only fifty miles per hour, and she juddered alarmingly when pushed to her maximum.

It was almost dark when Frank drove onto the boat. The yellow light inside beckoned him as if he were entering an alien spaceship, and to Frank it really was alien. For the first time in his life, he would be off British soil. In countries whose languages he couldn't speak a word of, and of whose cultures he had only the vaguest idea.

While he lay in his tiny cabin feeling queasy from the motion, he looked at the old atlas from the 1950s which he'd brought with him to serve as his roadmap. Frank marvelled at how once he reached Europe, he could go all the way to China, Siberia or India. In Britain, a few hundred miles was the farthest you could travel. Now he could cover thousands of miles if he had a mind to. The largest unbroken landmass on the planet was less than a hundred miles away, and he was about to go there.

His imagination was interrupted by vomit in the back of his throat. He dropped the atlas on the floor and got down on his knees next to the toilet where he passed most of the night.

It was overcast and raining when he arrived on the Continent but Frank didn't care. He was just happy to get off the ship and no longer feel seasick.

Like many British people, he didn't think of Britain

as being part of Europe, even though it was. That small stretch of water had, and still has, a disproportionate effect on the nation's psyche.

Brunhild's wiper blades turned out to be worn, leaving streaks of water across the windscreen while he drove out of the port. Peering at the road signs, he saw one for Germany. It was only one hundred kilometres. Not much more than fifty miles, he calculated.

Frank's impression of Holland was that it was as flat as a pancake. No wonder Hitler was able to capture it so quickly. There were no natural features to slow him down.

The houses weren't that different to back home. However, he did like the dedicated bike lanes set back from the roads, and separated from them by a strip of grass. In England, you had to take your chances and cycle amongst the traffic hoping for the best.

CHAPTER 4

Frank was disappointed they didn't stamp his passport when he arrived in Holland. At the German border, they didn't even look at it. In fact, there was no border to speak of. No one stopped you, you just kept on going.

All he noticed was a sign saying "Willkommen in Deutschland", that he took to be welcome to Germany and "Gute Fahrt", which he didn't understand, though it made him chuckle like a schoolboy. He later found out that it meant 'have a good journey'.

Now on their famous autobahns, he kept to the inside lane after nearly being hit from behind when he pulled out to pass a truck travelling even more slowly than him. Frank had read about there being no speed limit. Yet he hadn't understood its significance until he experienced how quickly a speck in the rear-view mirror could be right on your tail, hooting and flashing, and so close it seemed that the driver wanted to play bumper cars.

Deciding he was in no particular hurry, and

that Germany from the autobahn looked much the same as England, Frank took the next exit and motored along the ordinary roads. From this perspective, Germany was a lot different to England. Everything was so neat and tidy, not a piece of litter visible anywhere. And there seemed to be no dereliction, no wastelands of abandoned industrial sites, or unloved housing estates with broken cars and vandalised playgrounds like in Frank's hometown.

Even though it was a Saturday afternoon, the shops in the towns which he'd passed through were all shut. It was over twenty years since that had been the case at home. Not that it mattered. He had stocked the van with bread, eggs, tinned food and long-life milk. Gayle was right about his view of foreign food.

He stopped to put on the earphones of the Walkman Dawn had given him. Listening to Frank Sinatra's "My Way", he sang along as if he'd spent his entire life taking chances and doing exactly what he wanted, just like the character in the ballad. When the tape and his off key singing ended, he turned down a country lane and parked. Resolving to stay there for the night, Frank set about cooking himself egg on toast. A siren and flashing lights caught his attention as did the sign 'Polizei' on the car which stopped in front of Brunhild. Frank opened the door and stepped outside in response to the impatient knock.

"English?" said the policeman who had probably

noticed the GB sticker on the rear of the van.

"Yes."

"Camping here is prohibited. You must find a campsite."

"Sorry, I didn't realise."

"Well, now you know."

The officer waited, his arms akimbo. Frank threw away his meal and departed. Seeing a sign for a campsite a few miles later, he followed it and turned off down a dusty track.

"One night or longer?" asked a young man sitting in a wooden hut by the barrier at the entrance. Frank thought he looked rather underdressed for work. He was bare chested.

"One."

Frank paid the required amount.

"Don't forget to take your clothes off."

Frank wondered if he had misheard, or whether the man's English wasn't very good. Those were the last words he was expecting to hear. Noticing Frank's look of confusion, the man explained.

"We're part of Freikoeperkultur, the free body movement. It's on the sign as you come in."

Panic took hold of Frank and he began to sweat. It was exactly like Gayle had predicted. He'd seen the 'Frei' whatever it was sign, but that had meant nothing to him. Looking in his rearview mirror, he could see a line of cars waiting behind him. Frank was stuck and he'd already paid.

He could just stay inside his van, he reasoned. Dash across to the toilet block after dark and leave first thing in the morning. Keep a low profile. No one need see him. Frank was British after all, addicted to saying 'sorry' and embarrassed by most things, especially the human body.

Driving over to a spot under a large tree, he observed the casual unconsciousness of his fellow guests, totally uninhibited while they wandered around letting it all hang loose. He assumed that growing up, they must never have experienced nightmares about going to school not fully dressed. Certainly not those whose bits were bouncing around while they played volleyball.

Self-consciously, Frank undressed. Moving about the van, he kept low down. Then having a better idea, he closed the pink curtains. When he'd had Brunhild repainted blue, he hadn't changed them. There seemed no point. He was only expecting to use them when it was already dark.

His solution wasn't perfect, however. There were no curtains on the windscreen or the windows of the front doors. Frank would just have to hide in the rear of the van.

Dozing off on the sofa, he awoke to the sound of excited chatter outside. He heard the word 'Barkas' being repeated. His hopes to remain incognito were ruined. Two naked middle-aged couples were standing in front of the windscreen and enthusiastically waving at him. They'd already spotted him cowering in the back.

He had no choice but to go and open the door. Frank stood there bent over and with his hands strategically positioned in front of him.

"We were fascinated to see you have a Barkas," said one of the men in perfect English. "I'm Helmut."

He extended a hand, obliging Frank to step down and remove one of his hands from their modesty preserving position to shake Helmut's hand.

"How did you acquire one? You don't often see them."

"I bought it back home off a lady from Sweden."

"May we come in? We'd love to see inside one."

"I…"

Before Frank could think of an excuse, they were inside talking in German and laughing. He was worried by what they might touch and with what. In the narrow confines of the camper van, their buttock cheeks collided as they passed each other. Frank said 'sorry' repeatedly. He took some comfort from the fact it could have been much worse if they had been facing each other.

"It's very nice," said Helmut as he exited with his wife and the other couple. Frank, still not knowing quite where to look, kept his gaze resolutely at head height.

"You must come dine with us this evening. We're over there," said Helmut pointing. "See you at seven. And don't be embarrassed, we all have the same bits. Well, at least half of us do."

Frank had no time to refuse before they were gone. If only Gayle could see him now, she'd probably wet herself with laughter.

He decided he couldn't avoid a visit to the camp

shop. He needed to buy some wine to take, it would be rude not to.

"Do you have any Blue Nun?" Frank asked the server, who he was relieved to see was a middle-aged man, not some beautiful woman.

"No, we send it to you English. It's too downmarket for us."

Frank was surprised. He'd always thought it the height of sophistication when he and Gayle had drunk a bottle with their Sunday lunch. He wondered if the Black Forest gateau which Gayle used to buy for dessert at the supermarket on special occasions was also sneered at by Germans.

"I can recommend that wine over there."

Frank bought it. Carrying the bottle as though it were a loincloth, he made his way over to the wooden picnic table where Helmut and the others were already seated, drinking. Helmut made the introductions.

"This is my wife, Johanna, and Hans and his wife, Frieda."

"Hello, I'm Frank."

"Please sit."

With relief, Frank sat down on the bench and handed Helmut the bottle of wine. He was next to Frieda who had shuffled along to make room for him.

"Ouch!"

"Is everything okay?" she asked.

"A splinter, I think."

"Stand up and let me have a look."

"That won't be necessary. I'm fine."

To him, it was bad enough to be sitting naked with these people without having her explore his bare backside for a tiny piece of wood.

"So what brings you here, Frank?" asked Hans. "We don't get many English visitors in this part of Germany."

"I'm travelling around to see a bit of Europe."

"In a Barkas, no less. You're the talk of the camp."

Frank wished that he wasn't. He would have liked nothing better than to go unnoticed.

"You're the first Englishman I've met who enjoys nudity," said Johanna.

"Oh that, not really. I thought it was an ordinary campsite."

His confession produced howls of laughter.

"Here, have some wine."

Helmut poured him a generous glass.

"Cheers."

"In Germany, we say 'Prost'."

"Prost," repeated Frank.

"You can come help Hans and me at the bar-b-q. Only be careful, don't get too close and burn your you know what."

The others laughed heartily.

"I won't thanks, I'm a terrible cook."

He was, but more importantly it would mean standing up.

"You're a funny guy, Frank," said Helmut.

Still not knowing where to look while the women left the table and came to and fro bringing bread and salad, Frank relaxed a little when everyone was finally seated and eating.

Downing plenty of wine, he didn't refuse later when they asked him to go swimming with them in the lake. By then it was dark and the camp lighting was dim, sparing his blushes. It was the best fun he could recall having in years. He had to admit it felt much better than swimming with a bathing costume on. It was so much freer and cold water shrinkage was a great equaliser.

CHAPTER 5

The next morning, Frank was extremely glad to put his clothes back on once he was ready to depart. His new friends were there to see him off.

"Make sure you come and visit us if you find yourself near Stuttgart. You have our address. We've all seen each other naked so there's nothing to hide anymore," said Johanna.

"I will."

But Frank had no intention of visiting them. Yet he did drive off with a broad grin on his face. This travel lark was turning out to be more enjoyable than he had anticipated, although he'd probably omit the nudist camp from his holiday stories when he got home. They'd only call him a 'perv' or a 'dirty old man' down at the Queen Mary.

He made his way south to Rothenburg ob Der Tauber in Southern Germany, a place his new friends had highly recommended. From the road, he carefully scrutinised the campsite he'd chosen to ensure that its inhabitants were fully clothed before he entered.

Later, he walked into town. The recommendation

had been a good one. Rothenburg was a sheer delight. It was as though he had walked into a Brothers Grimm fairytale film set. He wouldn't have been surprised if he met Hansel and Gretel or saw Rapunzel calling for rescue from a tower.

Inside the sturdy town walls, which were topped by a slate roof and occasional towers, there were timbered buildings, all immaculately painted and preserved with steep sloping ochre coloured roofs. The most magnificent building was the Rathaus, or town hall as Frank discovered from the leaflet he'd picked up. The gothic double-fronted, gable-end building dominated the market square, rising several storeys.

Tourist crowds filled the streets and shops selling Christmas decorations all year long were numerous. A little kitsch it most certainly was, and probably an inspiration for Walt Disney, but Frank couldn't help liking it. Its dark past of being promoted as the perfect German town by the Nazis, and the inhabitants' eagerness in rounding up Jews for sending to concentration camps, was now confined to the history books.

Fortuitously, Frank had arrived during the beer festival. Bavarian jollity overflowed with many German men dressed in their lederhosen and women in their dirndls as if the place had been taken over by 'the Sound of Music' appreciation society. They were as blissfully unselfconscious in their garb as the nudists at his first campsite were about their lack of clothing.

Back home, Morris Men dancing around in their black hats, white shirts, and trousers decorated with bells and ribbons were considered a little odd. Here in Germany, their own tradition was celebrated by all with relish and admiration. A large oompah band belted out lively music. Frank positioned himself on the end of a long bench with his stein of beer. The large froth on top left him with a white moustache after he took a mouthful.

His neighbour, while not having such good English as last night's dining companions, knew enough to converse.

"Vot do you zink of our cuisine," asked a man about Frank's age who was wearing a green hat with a feather in it as well as green lederhosen and a white shirt.

"I wouldn't say I've eaten any proper German food yet."

"You must."

There were no coulds or maybes in Germany. Everything was definite and without doubts of any kind.

"Ve have zree hundred breads and over ein thousand types of sausage."

The man caught the eye of a passing waitress, and within minutes Frank found himself obliged to consume the longest sausage which he had ever seen in his life. The ends of it hung limply out of either end of the bread roll.

"Ver do you go next?" asked the man.

"I'd like to see East Germany."

"You don't vant to go zer, it's backvard. Difficult to get across, too. From communist countries I zink so but not from here."

"Excuse me, I just need to find the gents," said Frank standing up.

"Are you going big or small?"

Frank couldn't hide his astonishment.

"Don't vorry. It's a normal qvestion for us. Ve Germans are very direct."

"A little," answered Frank in that typically understated British way.

When he returned, the crowd were in full voice. His hand was grabbed the moment he sat back down. Long lines of people swayed side to side, their arms in the air. Frank wondered what they might be singing. 'We're all taking our tanks on a summer holiday', maybe. He was from the war generation who still viewed Germany through that prism.

Now being here, Frank was baffled such a beautiful country with friendly people could have allowed Nazism to thrive. Defeated in the First World War, Germany was required to pay reparations and handover land and industry. Hyperinflation and unemployment reduced the country to chaos. Hitler's message that he would restore stability and pride in being German seduced much of the population.

While he made his way back to his van later that evening, Frank laughed to himself as he thought how much he had emerged from his shell

GOING BIG OR SMALL?

these past two days. First nudity, and now public singing.

Back in Brunhild, he poured over his atlas trying to plan a route in the inadequate light of his torch. One of his many frustrations at ageing was how difficult it was to read in anything but the brightest of light.

According to measurements that he made with his fingers, it was only one hundred miles to Czechoslovakia and not far from there to East Germany. All he had to do was get through their border control.

CHAPTER 6

Crossing into Czechoslovakia proved to be relatively easy. The authorities there seemed keen on getting the western currency which Frank was forced to change for Czech koruna. In return, Frank got the first stamp in his passport which pleased him, even if it had cost a small fortune.

It was only an hour's drive along a potholed road until he reached the border with the German (so-called) Democratic Republic.

Frank didn't know much about the country, other than that it was the part of Germany which the Russians occupied at the end of the Second World War, and that there was a wall between it and West Germany, and also between East and West Berlin, which was completely surrounded by East Germany. American President John F. Kennedy had stood at the divide in Berlin famously saying "Ich bin ein Berliner", which many claim means "I'm a doughnut".

Frank also knew the country won an awful lot of medals at the Olympics. Last time, they came second only to the Soviet Union, even ahead of the USA, which was surprising for a country with a population less than one tenth of America's. The East German female athletes possessed very masculine physiques, and many suspected that the team took performance-enhancing drugs.

And, of course, Frank now knew it as the place that made the Barkas.

Much to Frank's relief, the Czech border guard spoke English.

"Do you have a visa to get in?"

"No, can't they give me one when I arrive?"

"You can't apply at the border. You would need to visit their embassy in Prague. And it takes a long while."

"Is there no other way?"

"Well," said the guard, checking the other one was still inside the hut hiding from the rain. "I know some of the guards over there. I could bribe them."

"What about getting back out?"

"They'd be happy to see you leave. There's no problem getting out unless you're East German. They say that wall they built was to keep out Western spies, but everyone knows it's to keep their people in. Just like our border fence with the West. You'll need some DDR registration plates."

"DDR?"

"Deutsche Demokratische Republik. East Germany to you. That way you won't get stopped moving around the country. I can get you some from a man I know. Meet me in town this evening by the park at six. You can't miss it. It'll cost you one hundred

Deutsch Mark, and you'll need another hundred to give to the guards at the DDR border post. Give me fifty now and the other fifty tonight."

Frank did the maths in his head. It was less than a hundred pounds. He wouldn't be passing this way again. The guard hadn't mentioned money for himself, but Frank was sure he would take his cut from the claimed cost of the number plates.

That evening, he parked by the park. Another vehicle arrived. The guard, now dressed in civilian clothes, produced the registration plates and helped him swop them with his British ones.

"Put your English ones back on when you're ready to leave East Germany. Come to the border at 13.00 tomorrow. My colleague will be on lunch break, and the two guards I know will be on the German side. Give them the money. They know you're coming."

"What about money when I'm there?"

"You can offer people West German Marks. They'll be delighted to take them. The official rate is one to one, but offer one West German Mark for ten East German Marks and most will accept that. Some might bargain a bit harder, but don't go higher than five East German Marks for one West German Mark."

That night, nervous excitement kept Frank awake. As the trip had progressed, he'd become ever less cautious, yet this was on a whole new level. At least all he had to do to get out again was change the number plates like the guard had explained.

GOING BIG OR SMALL?

The following day, having cleared the Czech border and crossing no man's land, apprehension wrapped itself around him like a boa constrictor. What if the guard was wrong?

Before Frank had time to change his mind, he reached the barrier on the other side which was already being raised. He drove under it. There was another barrier in front of him, and while the barrier behind him descended, Frank was caught between the two. No way back, no way forward.

A guard stepped out of the hut, a rifle slung over his shoulder. He appeared tense in comparison to his laid-back Czech counterpart. Standing by the driver's door, he motioned at Frank to get out.

"Nein! Nicht hier," he said, noticing Frank putting his hand in his pocket for the money. "Kommen Sie."

Frank followed him inside the hut, where a large photograph of Erich Honecker, the country's leader, hung on the wall. With his thin lips and narrow eyes, he reminded Frank of a villain in a James Bond film.

"Geld," said the guard pushing out his right hand, palm upward.

He counted what Frank gave him and passed half to his colleague in the hut who hadn't said a single word. Frank could hear his heart beating and was wishing he hadn't been so cavalier. He rubbed his hands together with nerves.

"Okay," said the guard jerking his head in the direction of the door.

"Can I go?"

"Ja."

While his clammy hands gripped the steering wheel, the barrier in front of Frank slowly lifted. Soon the border was behind him and his anxiety subsided.

Frank thought East Germany would look somewhat like West Germany. They were all Germans, after all. However, it appeared to be a country of unremitting dreariness. The older buildings were unpainted and crumbling with large chunks of plaster missing. The apartment blocks were uninspiring towers of concrete, some with gigantic pictures of Karl Marx and Lenin hanging from them. The roads were poorly maintained and shops notable for what they didn't have, rather than what they did have.

An enthusiastic member of the British Communist Party in his youth, Frank had expected to see more in a supposed workers' paradise, but it hadn't been a level playing field. West Germany received massive financial aid from the USA after the Second World War because America feared West German voters might favour communism if living standards remained low.

Russia took a different approach, demanding that East Germany pay reparations, and dismantled many of its factories and shipped them back to the Soviet Union. If the population rose up in protest at their poor conditions, the Union of Soviet Socialist Republics, the USSR, could just put tanks

GOING BIG OR SMALL?

on the streets and shoot protesters until order was restored, which is exactly what they did to squash an uprising in 1953.

Barkas vans were a common sight, which made Frank more relaxed that Brunhild would go unnoticed. She was nothing special here as she had been on the other side of the Iron Curtain.

They came in all different guises. They were in use by the fire service, with two flashing blue beacons and a ladder folded on the roof. They were also used as police vans and ambulances. Frank even noticed one sporting two ice cream cones on top. No one was buying, or maybe they had no ice cream to sell.

It didn't seem to be a country where you could spontaneously buy what you might happen to want that day. In West Germany, they told Frank that to buy a Trabant, East Germany's standard car, which looked as though it belonged in the 1950s, you had to wait over ten years. 'A spark plug with a roof' was how they had described the Trabant to him. Like Brunhild, Trabants were basic vehicles, but in a country without consumer choice they were what those who didn't have a car aspired to own.

Frank pressed on towards Berlin, a place he was excited to see given its pivotal role in twentieth century history. His plan was to take a quick look around before leaving for the western half of the city.

The man who he'd spoken to at the Bierfest in

Rothenburg told him that there were motorways out of there, paid for by West Germany which westerners used to get to and from West Berlin. 'Sealed corridors' so they didn't contaminate the mindset of those in the East. Albeit most of them were able to watch West German TV in the privacy of their homes and form their own judgment about which side of the wall they would rather be.

Reticent about using a campsite and not seeing any signs for any, Frank decided to spend the night off the road on a dirt track. He chose a spot where the van was partially obscured by low hanging tree branches. Whether it was his mind playing tricks or from watching too many spy

movies, he had by now convinced himself there was something sinister about this land as if he'd walked inside the pages of George Orwell's '1984'.

According to his atlas, Frank wasn't far from East Berlin. With an early start, he could be there by ten, do some sightseeing and cross into the safety of West Berlin during the afternoon.

A tap on the window as dusk was falling made him jump. A woman in a headscarf stood there. Her cheeks were rosy and her disposition friendly. Frank opened the door.

"Nicht Deutsch?" she said, noticing the blank look on his face in response to whatever she had said to him before that.

"English."

Her expression was as if he'd said he was a Martian. After looking furtively up and down the lane, she moved her hands up and down near her mouth indicating food, and then pointed her finger at him.

She turned to go. While Frank stood there hesitating, she twisted her head in his direction and made it clear that he should accompany her. She led him to a simple, single storey wooden house on the edge of the village. In reality, it was more like a barn than a dwelling.

Inside, the furniture was rudimentary and the place lit by a single dim lamp. There was a sheet hanging across the room. Frank assumed behind it must be the sleeping accommodation. Even though it was only early September, the place smelled damp and musty

A teenage girl was in a wheelchair, her head flopped over to one side and resting on her shoulder. A young man was seated on the one comfortable looking armchair. His mother spoke to him rapidly.

"We would like you to have dinner with us. Please, sit," he said rising from the chair and offering it to Frank.

"Thank you. You speak good English."

"I am studying it a long time now, on my own. In school, preference is given to Russian. It's compulsory. My name is Rudi."

"Frank. Pleased to meet you."

His mother spoke again to her son.

"She wants to know how an English person is here, and in a Barkas. We don't get visitors from the

West."

Frank explained he was traveling around Europe, leaving out the illegal border crossing into East Germany.

While his mother prepared dinner over a wood-fired stove, their conversation continued.

"We would like to travel. Move to West Germany. We could better care for my sister. Here disabled people have few opportunities. The government wants them kept separate from the able-bodied. They'd be happy for Mutti and Renate to go but they won't let me go, and Mutti refuses to leave without me.

"She can't work because she has to look after my sister. What I earned as a teacher wasn't much, and now I have been removed from my post so I get odd jobs where I can. The Party considers us subversive because we want to leave. Our neighbours shunned us for fear of being tainted by associating with us. We lost our apartment in town and were put here. As you can see, it's quite basic."

The mother placed soup on the table with a couple of dumplings floating in it, urging Frank to eat with another of her hand gestures. It smelled of little and tasted like hot water. While Frank and Rudi ate, she spoon fed Renate, who made occasional grunting sounds.

"Did anyone see you come here?"

"I don't think so."

"Good. The Stasi, that's the security police, keep

a close watch on everyone. You can't trust anybody. Many people work for the Stasi. They are everywhere, listening and watching."

Frank noticed the mother didn't eat anything. Feeling guilty that he must have eaten her portion, and humbled by their generosity, Frank pressed a hundred West German Marks into her hand as he left. She tried to give it back.

"Please tell her to keep it. Maybe she could get something Renate needs."

Mother and son spoke earnestly to each other.

"She says you are too kind."

"Your mother is too. Thank you for the meal. I hope you all get to West Germany one day soon."

Frank felt sad as he left them. He was on an adventure, able to observe other's misfortunes in comfort and enjoy the freedom of travel, something which they were denied.

Those allowed to visit West Germany to see family were required to leave behind a close relative, such as a child, to ensure their return. The East German government was more relaxed about

permitting the disabled or pensioners to leave because they were a burden on the country's finances.

Travel to 'the fraternal' socialist states of Eastern Europe was easier. East Germany was the most affluent of the communist nations, and those of its citizens who visited Russia were shocked at its low standard of living. They had been brought up to believe the Soviet Union was the most modern and progressive country in the world.

CHAPTER 7

When he approached Berlin the next day, Frank could see a tower on the skyline. Towards the top of it was an onion-shaped sphere and above that a long, thin spire stretched almost as far as the clouds above, or so it seemed. Rudi had told him about it. The tallest structure in Germany, the Fernsehturm, or TV tower, was a 'mine is bigger than yours' kind of thing. The East thumbing its nose at the West, and trying to convince its people of the East's economic success. 'Ulbricht's finger' (the name of the first East German leader) and 'Telesparagus' were two of its nicknames.

Assuming it was probably in the city centre, Frank used the landmark to navigate his way in closer until he was near. He arrived in a drab square around which stood unattractive apartment blocks. A massive, brown statue of Lenin towered high above the ground, built against a wall of the same stone. It was as though the man was about to leap into the air like some Communist superman to save the world.

Frank looked for a side street where other cars

were parked and pulled in. It wasn't a long walk until he reached the tower.

It too stood in a big open square, surrounded by bland socialist architecture. He was whisked up to the dome in one of the lifts. A hostess in a sky blue uniform explained its history and features and the sights below, first in German, then in Russian and lastly in English.

She enthusiastically described its designers as reaching for the stars. It did indeed look like some kind of rocket, though one from a comic book. Perhaps the authorities believed thoughts of space would take the population's mind off the fact that they couldn't even go a mile and a half down the road from here into West Berlin.

From the top, Frank could see the wall encircling West Berlin, or the 'Anti-Fascist Protection Rampart' as the guide so poetically described it. It was, in fact, two walls with a space in between, nicknamed the death strip. At regular intervals watchtowers stood, manned with soldiers ready to shoot if they saw anyone trying to escape to West Berlin. The guide didn't refer to any such sensitive matters. Everyone was allegedly happy and committed to the cause in this socialist paradise. Frank realised it was like falling down a rabbit hole. He had entered an Alice in Wonderland world.

Leaving the tower, he walked along Unter Den Linden, the heart of pre-war Berlin, towards the Brandenburg Gate. A triumphal arch on six Doric columns topped with the goddess of Victory on a four-horse drawn carriage, the Gate had been tainted by the Nazi parades which had marched through it. Now it was unused and the flag of East Germany flew from it, and soldiers goose-stepped in front of it. A sturdy metal fence kept him and other visitors well back.

Looking beyond the monument, he could see the concrete wall. Like a prisoner wanting to escape the confines of his cell, Frank was filled with a sudden urge to get out of the East as fast as possible. Walking back towards his car, Frank was fascinated to see numerous bullet holes in the older buildings, like stone faces pockmarked from acne. Damage from when the Russians took the city in 1945 which had still not been repaired all these years later.

Brunhild had acquired a friend. A cream coloured Barkas was parked next to her. Behind the front seats, it had been converted to a delivery truck without windows.

"Papiere," demanded a stern voice when Frank went to get in his van.

Turning, he saw two men dressed in grey uniforms and peak caps. They wore brown belts around the outside of their uniform at the top of their waists. Lacking only the Nazi emblem, it was as if Frank had been transported back to the Second World War.

"Papiere," repeated the man impatiently, his hand out awaiting them.

Frank had seen enough war films to know what he meant.

"I'm English, I'm only visiting and I'm about to leave. I'm going to Check Point Charlie right now." He tried not to sound nervous but failed.

"Show me your passport and visa," said the man in English.

Frank handed over his passport.

"Visa?"

"I don't have one."

"What do you mean you don't have one. How did you get in?"

Frank swallowed hard and broke out in a cold sweat. He didn't know what to say.

"Come with us."

One of them took Frank forcefully by the arm and opened a side door to their Barkas. Inside was a bench seat with red upholstery. He pushed Frank in and shut the door. There was no light and it was pitch black. Frank heard them exchange some words outside and then that familiar asthmatic rumble as the vehicle moved off.

A few minutes later his door was opened.

"Raus!" demanded a guard. Again Frank knew from films about the war what that meant.

He got out. They'd arrived in a high-walled courtyard in front of a drab building. He was grabbed by the arm once more and marched inside at speed and down a long corridor and then steered into a small room. There was a table with two chairs on opposite sides. Nothing else. It was completely bare, apart from a lightbulb dangling down from the ceiling which cast a harsh, accusatory light. They hadn't bothered to paint the walls. An interrogation room, there was no need to think about aesthetics.

Frank was pushed down onto a chair. His guards sat down on the other side.

"Who are you working for?" asked the one who had done the talking earlier.

"No one, I'm retired. A tourist."

"Don't try to be clever with me, Frank Braithwaite." There was the gravel of menace in the man's voice now.

"The British or the Americans?"

Frank wondered if he was in a parallel universe. How could they possibly think he was a spy? No one could surely look less like one than him with a circular bald patch in the middle of his head, grey in the hair which still remained, and small round National Health issue glasses with brown frames.

"Why do you have a Barkas and DDR registration plates with English plates hidden inside?"

"The guard at the Czech border got them for me. He told me to use them until I left."

The questioning continued for what seemed like hours. They wore him down, asking the same things time and again. Relentlessly, they bombarded him and Frank lost all track of time. Whether it was day or night, he had no clue. He was hungry, thirsty, and tired. He only wanted for it to stop.

"Why don't you confess to being a saboteur? A spy for the West."

"Because I'm not. I'm a pensioner on a trip around Europe. I've never left England before in my life. I was curious to see the country my vehicle came from. How could I possibly be a spy? I can't speak a word of German. I'm very sorry for coming in without a visa. I would just like to go now, please."

"Not until you confess."

"Okay, I'll say what you want if you'll let me go."

"Good. Now we're making progress. We'll prepare a paper for you to sign."

The man who had taken notes led him down a staircase. Frank guessed that they were now underground. Large pipes ran along the ceiling of a windowless corridor.

On both sides were closed grey metal doors. Opening one, the man pushed Frank inside and locked it. Like the interrogation room, a single bulb hung down illuminating the small cell. It couldn't have been more than two metres by two metres. A bed with a dirty mattress, an old blanket, and a bucket in one corner were the furnishings.

Frank thumped the wall with his hands for being so naive and entering the country illegally. He fervently hoped they would keep their word and let him go once he signed his confession. If not, who would ever know he was here in this silent underworld. They could leave him to rot if they wanted to, like a prisoner in a medieval oubliette.

The Stasi were the most effective and repressive

of all the Eastern bloc surveillance forces. With their informers, there was one for every six East German citizens. Neither the Nazis nor the KGB came anywhere close to that ratio. Everyone was monitored. Failing to denounce someone when you could have was also a crime. This was a Big Brother state on an unprecedented scale.

Exhausted, Frank lay down and fell asleep. When he awoke, some bread and water had been left. The bread was stale. Before he'd finished eating, the door opened and he was escorted back to the interrogation room.

This time a woman in uniform and with short, no nonsense blonde hair was seated with the guard who had taken notes yesterday.

"Did you sleep well?"

Her demeanour was almost friendly.

"Yes, thank you."

"Good. I have here your confession for you to sign."

She pushed a sheet of paper across the table. The only words Frank could read were his name.

"It's in German. I can't understand it."

"It says you were sent here by the British secret service as an agent to spy and report back."

"It seems much longer than that."

"It also describes how you were furnished with a Barkas, and came in using false vehicle number plates," she said handing him a pen.

"So if I sign it, I can go?"

"Once formalities are completed."

Frank signed. The woman spoke in German to the

notetaker who led Frank back to his cell.
"How long will it be?"
"I don't know," replied the guard.
"A day? Two days?"
The guard ignored his question and left.
What seemed like the next day, but could have been the one after that, Frank was escorted back to the interrogation room. The same woman was seated there. Finally, thought Frank, I'll be out of here.
"Sit."
Her tone was sharp and the lack of small talk made his pulse race.
"My superior has decided you are to be prosecuted."
"What do you mean? You said I'd be let go."
"It's not my decision any longer. It's out of my control."
Frank stood up and leaned forward, placing his hands on the table.
"This is ridiculous! You got me to sign a confession for something I didn't do. I demand to see a lawyer."
"The judge will decide such matters," she said in a monotone voice, ignoring Frank's anger. She nodded at the guards standing behind him who led him away.

CHAPTER 8

It was late summer when Frank arrived in East Germany. By Frank's reckoning it must be early November by now, although it was hard to be sure. Each day segued into another. Nothing ever happened to distinguish one from the next.

He remained imprisoned in the cell. There had been no judge and no trial. Nothing, other than a daily exercise in a walled compound. He was permitted to walk around the yard for a short while.

It was an unloved place. A few weeds pushed their way through the hard surface and leaves from trees on the other side of the wall had blown in. Brown and crinkled, they flew around near the ground in the wind like dying moths. To Frank, they were a metaphor for what his life had become. He was in the autumn of his life, wasting away here. His last chance to enjoy his life was slipping away as the last leaves fell and the winter beckoned, calling with an unwelcoming chill.

Recent days had been cold but sunny. The blue sky cheered him a little and took the focus away from the barbed wire around the top of the wall. Other prisoners walked there too, heads down, each lost in a solitary world. Conversation was forbidden, enforced by their jailers who stood against the brick walls chain-smoking. A nasty odour filled the air, an acrid smell from the cheap lignite used everywhere in East Germany for heating fuel.

Frank was allowed to shower twice a week, and given communist propaganda to read. But ever lasting friendship with Cuba, or exceeding the quota at the tractor factory plant hardly made for a riveting read.

He wondered if any of his family were trying to find him. Though even if they were, how could they? He hadn't left a trail for anyone to follow. Frank had become a non-person. He no longer existed and couldn't be traced. If he'd been a spy, the British government would know that he was missing, and he could have been expected to be released at some point as part of a prisoner exchange. But Frank was a nobody. He really had disappeared down that rabbit hole.

Any questions he asked were answered with "'Soon", "Be patient" or "Ich spreche kein Englisch" (I don't speak English). He felt like a prisoner of war, but even they had been allowed to mingle with each other. Frank was alone in his cell, no fellow compatriots to talk to and help keep up his spirits. He missed the sharp wit, sarcasm, and grumbling of the men at his local pub.

One evening, or Frank assumed it was, the door

opened. He had eaten dinner if that is what the awful slop they served here could be described as and fallen asleep on the bed. As always, Frank had tried not to move from that one position where the springs in the mattress weren't quite so prominent. Shielding his eyes from the bright light in the corridor outside, at first all he could make out was a woman's silhouette.

"Come."

He got up and followed. It was the officer who had presented him with his confession.

"What's going on?"

"Keep quiet and follow me."

She led him briskly out of the main door to the corridor and up the stairs. What could they possibly want from him now?

To his surprise, he wasn't taken to an interrogation room but out to the car park. Was he being moved to some other jail, a gulag maybe or whatever the East German equivalent was? Or were they just going to take him off and shoot him? Throw him in some unmarked grave? Beads of sweat formed on his forehead and his temples thrummed. His mind raced with the possibilities, none of which seemed good.

To his astonishment, the woman took him over to Brunhild which was parked alone in a corner.

"Get in."

Frank hesitated. What if they were setting him up? Making it look like he had tried to escape so they could open fire on him.

"Get in, now."

This time, she pushed him. Inside, Brunhild was exactly as he'd left her. The woman got in too.

"They've opened the Wall. I'm going to drive you out of here. I want you to hide in the storage cupboard under the sofa at the back."

"Opened the Wall?"

"I don't have time to explain."

She pulled out the duvet from the cupboard and Frank did as he was told. He lay down and slid in in an awkward manner, like a seal on land.

"Here, take these."

She gave him the English number plates, and then pushed the duvet back in. The engine stuttered to life. After a short way, they stopped. He could hear the woman talking to the guard at the entrance. Frank lay perfectly still, his heart beating rapdily.

Off they moved again. Frank wondered if he was dreaming and would soon wake up back in prison. Cut off from the outside world, he knew nothing of the events unfolding. Protests against the regime had been building in recent weeks. Only a few days earlier, half a million people gathered near the TV Tower in Alexanderplatz demanding change. The Russian President, Mikhail Gorbachev, hadn't ordered the East German government to intervene to squash the demonstrations as previous Russian leaders would have done.

After a few minutes, the van stopped. The woman lifted the wooden flap.

"Come out."

"Have we crossed the wall?"

"No. Here's your passport in case you need it. A government spokesman went on TV earlier to announce a relaxation in border crossing rules. When asked when they became effective, he said immediately. They say thousands are gathering at the exit points, demanding to cross and the guards are letting them through. You should be okay. I will now hide in case they're not letting Stasi through."

"But what if we're caught?"

"I can take you back to the prison if you would prefer," she said, irritation in her voice.

"No, I'd rather take my chances."

"Me too. My brother claimed sanctuary in the West German embassy in Prague last month along with thousands of others. They were put in sealed trains which were allowed to cross East Germany and enter into West Germany. General Secretary of the Party, Honecker, named them traitors and stripped them of their citizenship. I'm now under suspicion because of my brother. When I heard the Wall was open, I decided to get out. There's no guarantee it will stay open. The government could easily change its mind, or the Russians might order their tanks onto the streets and start shooting the people. It's happened before."

"Which way do I go?" asked Frank

"Left at the end of the street and keep going straight."

Frank's mouth was as dry as sandpaper when he approached border control. A long line of red lights stretched in front of him. Ossies (the East Germans) in their highly polluting Trabants queued nose to tail, their occupants hoping to do something which they never thought they would be able to.

The traffic moved slowly, but it kept on moving. He could see the raised barrier now. He watched it, fearful that it might go down. Miraculously, it didn't. The border guards stood around chatting, ignoring the mass exodus.

One looked up and saw Frank staring at them. He raised his arm. Frank cursed for having attracted the soldier's attention.

CHAPTER 9

The soldier waved him through. Frank's shoulders fell in relief, they weren't going to be stopped after all.

In a few moments, they had crossed the strip of land where during the last three decades many had been shot dead for trying to do what Frank and thousands of others were doing tonight. Until 1961, there was no barrier, but with as many as five thousand East Germans defecting to West Berlin every day, East Germany had been haemorrhaging its people. One August night that year, barbed wire was rolled out like a massive cage while people slept, and the Wall followed soon afterwards.

In only one night that barrier, which had divided families for nearly thirty years, was now breached, a dam bursting from the pressure of the collective desire of an entire people to get out of their own country.

Entering West Berlin was like arriving at a New Year's party in full swing. Ossies were getting out of their cars into the embrace of Wessies (West

Germans) to the sounds of cheering and applause, and a popping of corks. The two tribes greeted each other like long-lost relatives as indeed many of them were.

Frank could see people climbing onto the hated Wall and helping others up. Waving flags and chanting, some began to chip away at it with hammers and other tools. On this side, it was plastered with graffiti, something those in the East would never have dared do.

A realisation hit Frank that he was watching history being made. Should anyone ever ask him in future if he remembered the fall of the Berlin Wall, he could proudly say "Remember it? I saw it happen. I was there."

Frank hadn't fought in the Second World War. His factory was deemed too important to the war effort and so he was ordered to keep working there, supervising the female workforce brought in to cover the men away fighting. He always felt awkward when war stories were exchanged by those who had gone away to fight, especially when his turn came to say what he did during the war. Now he would have a tale to tell to take attention away from all that.

Once past the throng of people gathered by the Wall, Frank pulled over and opened the storage cupboard.

"We're through."

"I can hear. The West is so noisy. Many of my fellow citizens think it's a utopia. I think they may be disappointed once they truly get to know it."

Now on her feet, his rescuer gave Frank an unexpected kiss.

"Good luck, Frank."

"And you too. And thanks."

"Auf Wiedersehen."

"Hey, I don't even know your name."

"It's better that way," she called out, already disappearing into the crowds.

Frank rejoined the traffic while it crawled along past the bright lights of West Berlin, horns honking and people shouting joyfully at each other. It was as if the Ossies had left the confines of the monastery and burst into a nightclub. This half of the city lived by a very different beat, pulsating like a disco. Its pervasive neon lights were a sharp contrast to the sparse lighting on the other side of the Wall.

Not everyone was thrilled by the events unfolding that night, including a KGB officer then in his thirties stationed in Dresden. He considered the failure of the authorities to clamp down hard had allowed things to spiral out of control. Showing weakness of any kind he believed to be a serious misjudgment. The experience of that night and what followed, including the collapse of the Soviet Union only two years later, would shape his views for the rest of his life. His name was Vladimir Putin.

Seeing the bright yellow 'M' of a McDonalds, Frank parked and filled himself on a Big Mac and fries. Never a fan at home, considering that their offerings tasted so much less good than they smelled, and bore little relation to the photos. However, tonight, after weeks of poor food at 'Hotel Stasi', a Big Mac tasted delicious.

Driving Brunhild into a side street that seemed not to have been invited to Europe's biggest rave in living memory, Frank gratefully pulled out the bed and slept in comfort for the first time since September. He was out, he was free again. What a wonderful and unexpected surprise.

Frank's world had reopened, and he was still high on excitement the following morning. In a spirit of adventure, Frank bought a currywurst, the West Berlin love affair for eating sausage with curry sauce on it. Standing on the street corner while he ate, Frank noticed a sign for the motorway to Hanover in West Germany.

He resolved to give the sights of West Berlin a miss and press on. Who knew what was going to happen here next? He didn't want to find himself stranded, unable to get away, should the Russians have a change of heart and seal off the city like they had in the past. As a Russian leader, Nikita Khrushchev, once put it:

"Berlin is the testicles of the West. When I want to make the West scream, I squeeze Berlin."

The motorway was poorly maintained, even though the West German government paid millions each year to the East to allow Westerners to travel along it. Frank was stopped crossing out of West Berlin, and at the West German border as well as a checkpoint along the way, but only for cursory glances at his passport. Perhaps the East German guards already sensed their jobs may soon disappear and couldn't be bothered any longer to perform them with the Teutonic doggedness they'd once shown.

Frank whooped with joy as he crossed into West Germany. He was delighted to be back in the land of the 'Gute Fahrt'. Finding a campsite, he spent a quiet evening contemplating what to do next.

Imprisoned in Berlin, he'd wanted nothing more than to go home. Now, reunited with Brunhild, he wasn't so sure. What would he be going back to? The same old, same old. He liked life on the road; well, not his stay with the Stasi, but the rest of it. Each day seeing somewhere new, something different.

At times, he wished there was someone to share his journey with, but he was used to being alone. He'd met many nice people along the way, and would doubtless meet more. There was so much of Europe still left to see.

He would write to Dawn to say that he wouldn't be coming home yet. He would instead go south in search of a warmer winter.

Sitting with his trusty atlas and his duvet draped over his shoulders to keep warm, he considered where to go. He ruled out Greece. That would mean driving through Yugoslavia. Frank had had his fill of communist countries, even if it was supposed to be more liberal than the others. He would aim for Italy or Spain by way of France.

Frank noted Stuttgart wasn't far from the French border. He could meet up with Helmut and Johanna on the way and see more of Germany before he got there. His memories of naked embarrassment had faded sufficiently.

"You must come and stay with us," insisted Johanna when he rang from a public phone box the day before his arrival.

Their house was in a picture postcard perfect village on the edge of the Black Forest. The outside of their home was equally cute, all dark wood and white paint.

"I didn't recognise you with your clothes on," laughed Johanna when Frank arrived.

Frank became hot and realised he must be blushing.

"Oh, you British, you have such a hang up with the human body. It's nothing to be ashamed of. But don't worry, we'll keep our clothes on while you're here."

Frank looked at all of her. Something which he had felt unable to do when they first met. She must have been about fifty. Her hair was cut short. It seemed to be the German fashion. She was wearing a green sweater and cream coloured slacks and her face was round and cheerful.

"Come, let me show you to your room. Helmut's in Frankfurt on business. He'll be home tomorrow evening."

GOING BIG OR SMALL?

Inside the house everything was in pine; the walls, the floor, the table, and the chairs. It was as if they lived inside a tree. While Johanna led him up the pine staircase, the sound of mechanical birds filled the house.

"Cuckoo clocks. We have fifteen, I collect them. I've turned the one in your room off, so it doesn't wake you in the middle of the night. They don't bother us, but we're used to them. I'll leave you to get settled. Come down when you're ready."

Frank sat down on the bed. The duvet was so big and soft, he was sure he would have a good night's sleep. He remembered how modern duvets once seemed. Until they converted to the European way in the 1970s, Britons slept under sheets and blankets, often tucked in so tightly that it was both hard to move and to keep out the cold air which invariably found its way in through the gaps between the top of the sheets and the body.

Through the small window, Frank could see the russet-tiled roofs of other chocolate box cover houses. Beyond were hills, whose lower slopes were covered by vineyards and whose upper slopes were forested.

"Let's go eat," said Johanna the moment he came downstairs. "I'll take you to a Weinstube."

They descended a street of other perfectly maintained old timbered houses with shutters of green or red. Frank half expected to see Chitty Chitty Bang Bang land at any moment. Even though he had been back in West Germany for a few days, he was still impressed with how clean and orderly everything was. How was it, he wondered, that the country which lost the war looked so much more prosperous and better kept than the victor? Where had England gone wrong?

The Weinstube was located in the basement of a large old building in the village square. The cellar was a series of arches. Subtle lighting gave a snug atmosphere while they tucked into plates of sliced meats and cheeses, washed down with the local red and white wines chosen by Johanna.

"Where do you go next, Frank?"

"France, then Spain or Italy."

"How wonderful. I should come with you."

"Why would you ever want to leave this idyllic spot?"

"Because I have spent my entire adult life here being the typical German Hausfrau. The beauty and perfection can be a little claustrophobic at times. You're not the only middle-aged person yearning for adventure. I dream of taking a big camper van across North America. A 'Thelma and Louise' type of trip."

"But didn't they die driving off a cliff and into a canyon?"

"Yes, but what a wonderful way to go when the alternative is a slow deterioration. How do you want to die, Frank? Live until you fall apart and sit peeing yourself in an old people's home, or go out with a bang. I know which I'd prefer."

"To be honest, I'd never really thought of it like

that."

"Well, you should. Old age creeps up on us without us noticing until it's too late to make our own choices."

"Suicide you mean?" asked Frank.

"I think of it as choosing to leave this life on your own terms. Not being kept alive just for the sake of it."

Frank quaffed some more wine. "Well, that's certainly food for thought. What do you think about all that's happening in East Germany?"

Johanna placed her hand in front of her mouth as if wondering whether to share. Then looking around to check no one was watching them, she leaned forwards.

"For most people it is good. For me, it's a worry."

"Why?"

"I have family there. My mother and two brothers. I came across as a teenager in the fifties, before the Wall was built."

"Well, now you can get to see them."

"Yes, that is true."

"You don't seem very excited at the prospect."

Her voice descended to a whisper. "The Stasi compromised me. They tracked me down years ago and blackmailed me into working for them, spying for them. They told me things would go badly for my family if I didn't co-operate. Now I worry if that will all come out, the records about their agents in the West. And if I would be prosecuted."

"What did you do?"

"I was a secretary at the American airbase. I passed on information to my contact."

"Oh God."

"Yes, you're right, oh God. I'm not really sure why I've told you all this. It must be too much wine. It's time to go back to the house. I have some excellent schnapps and if we drink anymore here, we'll trip over the cobbles."

Which is exactly what Frank did as they made their way back up the steep hill.

"You must hold my hand from now on," commanded Johanna.

Back at the house, she sat him down on the checked red and white cushions which covered the bench seat running along two sides of the dining table while she went to pour them some schnapps. Frank didn't remember how many he had before the room started to spin. Nor did he remember how he got himself upstairs into bed, and why he should now be naked under his duvet with Johanna snuggled up next to him.

CHAPTER 10

Johanna's body was enticingly soft and warm but Frank was startled nonetheless.

"Don't look so frightened, Frank. I don't bite," laughed Johanna.

"But what about Helmut?"

"We have an open marriage. Kiss me."

She placed her lips on his. Frank pulled away.

"There's no need to feel guilty. He has his girlfriends."

"But I do feel guilty. I've never done anything like this before."

"Well, isn't it about time? Life isn't a rehearsal, you only get one chance."

"I'm sorry, I really should go."

"Sorry? Why do you British always have to apologise for things which don't merit an apology."

"It's been an experience," said Frank as he got out of bed and began dressing.

"An experience! You're as bad as a German. French and Italian men, now they know how to charm a woman."

"Goodbye, Johanna, and thank you for... for everything."

"Goodbye, Frank," she called down the stairs after him. He stumbled in his haste. "Be careful. And don't forget to call if you decide you want company or you get into trouble and need help."

Reaching Brunhild, Frank realised the effects of the alcohol hadn't worn off completely and that he must still be over the limit. Concentrating hard, Frank risked it and drove out of the village a few miles before stopping down a side road.

It was already dark so he decided to chance it and stay the night. It was unlikely that the police would be coming down this road. But Frank had forgotten about German thoroughness. Not long after he had settled under his duvet, there was a vigorous knocking on the window. This officer spoke no English.

"Verboten," he kept repeating. He wrote on a piece of paper, which he tore from a notebook and gave to Frank. "Einhundert."

Frank could see the number one hundred. He rummaged in his trouser pockets. He only had fifty Marks.

"No more. Need bank. Tomorrow?"

"Nein. Folgen mir."

The policeman returned to his car, indicating with his emphatic arm movements that Frank was to follow behind in Brunhild. Arriving behind the flashing lights in a small town, Frank felt extremely conspicuous.

He parked in front of the police station. After surrendering his passport and being fingerprinted, he was led into a cell. Unlike East Berlin, this one was spotlessly clean and the bed was comfortable, but it was still a cell.

Frank regretted leaving Johanna's. He could have been safe and sound, and more. He would have been sleeping with a Cold War spy. Now that was a story Frank could have impressed the men down at the Queen Mary with when he got home, although they probably wouldn't believe him. Straight-laced Frank, suddenly transformed into a lothario. They would just laugh and tell him to pull the other one.

The next morning, another officer who spoke English unlocked the door of his cell and led him into the public area.

"You need to go to the bank and get two hundred marks. There's one opposite here."

"Two hundred?"

"Yes, the fine is double because you didn't pay immediately."

"I'll need my wallet."

"It's there on the counter."

The officer pointed, distracted by the ringing phone which he answered.

Not only Frank's wallet but also his passport and car keys lay on the counter. Should he? The man had his back to him now and was engrossed in conversation.

Feeling as if he were Steve McQueen in 'The

Great Escape', Frank grabbed his things and walked out. Brunhild was still parked out front. Looking around, Frank couldn't see anyone watching.

Brunhild coughed loudly when Frank turned the keys in the ignition, giving the West a good dose of pollution from the East as black exhaust smoke poured from her. Reversing, Frank swung her around and headed out of town towards the French border as fast as he could manage. No more boring, predictable Frank. He was a changed man. Well, maybe.

Following signs for Strasbourg, he soon found himself in that city. After parking, he walked across the medieval bridge with towers on it and into the old town. Quaint timbered old houses were everywhere. It was as if he was still in Germany. That was no coincidence. This part of Europe yo-yoed between France and Germany for hundreds of years, most recently returning to France after the First World War.

In the main square stood an enormous Christmas tree. Traders were opening their wooden huts at the Christmas market. Frank decided to spend a leisurely day here before moving on. Being the 1980s, the idea of European style Christmas markets hadn't yet caught on in Britain, at least where Frank came from.

He was charmed by the sights and smells, especially the enticing smell of vin chaud, or Gluhwein. After a couple of glasses, he was in need of an afternoon nap. Working his way through the streets to the Gothic cathedral, using its spire as his guide, he slipped inside and sat gratefully down on a pew a couple of rows from the back. Reading the English version of the tourist leaflet, he soon nodded off, though not before learning that it had been the world's tallest building until the 1870s.

When he awoke, all was in shadow save for candlelight at intervals down the sides. At the front, a choir was singing carols. Frank remained for a while letting the music soothe him. However, melancholy descended on him like a damp fog when he remembered he would be spending Christmas all alone on the road somewhere.

Thinking of how the festive season was these days soon snapped him out of that mood. Life had made him Scrooge-like at Christmas. It had become a time to get through, no longer a time to cherish. The big family gatherings of yesteryear had become a memory as relatives had passed on and children had grown up. Somewhere along the way, the magic had died.

Having to listen to Gayle prattle on about her and Morris's latest extravagant purchases or world travels made him feel inadequate. And when they asked Frank what he'd been up to, he never had anything interesting to tell them. It all left him rather depressed.

Yet perhaps it was Gayle's travel stories which had finally galvanised him into doing something and coming to Europe. Life is what you choose to make it and he knew that he had been a miserable git for a long time.

Outside, though the sky was a dark indigo. Cheery lights and the warm glow of shops called to him with their attractive displays. He had to hand it to the French, they knew how to dress a window. In the Christmas market, he bought a couple of wooden toys which they wrapped for him. He would post them to his grandchildren tomorrow.

Reaching Brunhild, he swore. There was a paper in plastic wrapping stuck behind his wiper blades. But then, so what, he thought. Like the Germans, what could they do? They could whistle for his parking ticket. He would be out of the country in a few days, long before he was due to pay the fine.

However, even though he was in the land that gave us the expression 'laissez-faire', Frank decided he better find a campsite for the night. Already knowing more about German prisons than he wanted to, he had no desire to try out a French one should roadside camping be illegal in France also.

Consulting his atlas that evening, he plotted his route south. He would keep on going until he met the Mediterranean and turn right to Spain. Millions of pallid Britons who flocked to the Costas each year couldn't be wrong. And at this time of year, Frank wouldn't have to worry about turning into a lobster like he did if he ever sat in the summer sun at home.

As France revealed more of herself, he discovered that she was nothing like Germany. The slightly oppressive perfection of that country had given way to a land where exterior painting wasn't a national obsession. Old buildings were generally untouched, left as grey plaster or grey stone. Certainty and uniformity had surrendered to a bit of anarchy, especially when it came to their driving.

"You silly bugger!" yelled Frank the first few times he drove through small towns when Citroen 2CVs and other cars which only the French could have designed, came whizzing out of side roads. Their drivers neither slowed down or even looked. Enquiring one day at a cafe where the waitress spoke English, he found out why.

"Priorité à droite," she explained. "You must give way to traffic coming from the right. Look out for the diamond-shaped signs, a yellow one in a white one. If there is a black line through it, you must give way. You don't have priority."

Now Frank knew, he approached each side road joining the main road with caution. But it baffled him. Who could have thought such a rule made sense?

In France, Frank struggled to converse most of the time. Almost everyone had spoken English in West Germany. Here almost everyone didn't or if they did, they didn't let on. Communication on the part of the French was generally limited to a shrug of the shoulders, and a throwing of the palm of the hands out from the body at chest height as if Frank were from the planet Zog.

In the end, it wasn't a car that drove Frank off the road as it came careering out of a back street but a person leaping out in front of him like a wild Dervish, arms waving furiously as France meandered along a rural road one wet December afternoon somewhere south of Lyon.

CHAPTER 11

Frank cursed and swerved. He had been far away, enjoying a Louis Armstrong trumpet solo on his Walkman. Brunhild skidded to a halt amongst grapevines, which at this time of year were a tangle of gnarled branches.

Frank was shocked but unhurt. While he sat there recovering, there was an insistent banging on his passenger window. A woman, her hair plastered down by the rain, and her mascara running like rivulets of dirt down her face, was demanding his attention.

"Mon Dieu," she exclaimed as she opened the passenger door and climbed in without being asked. Frank removed his headphones.

"What the hell do you think you were doing jumping out in front of me like that?"

"Oh, you're English." She sounded unimpressed.

"Yes. You didn't answer my question. Is that how you hitchhike in France?"

"I wanted to make sure you stopped."

"Well, you succeeded. And Brunhild's as good as fermenting wine now."

"Brunhild?"

"My camper van."

"You English are so eccentric. I really don't know how you managed to conquer half the world. I'm Delphine. Can you drive me into town." It wasn't said as a question, more as a command. "I'll buy you a coffee for your trouble."

Delphine was dressed in an expensive looking red, though very damp dress. Frank had been in France long enough now to know that tracksuit bottoms, ill-fitting tops and trainers weren't part of the national dress like in his town. Like nearly all French women, she was thin. No middle-aged spread here as in England.

"All right, I could do with a drink after nearly running you over," he said, reversing back onto the road. "Why on earth are you out here in the middle of nowhere? And without a coat on such a horrible day."

"Did you see that chateau back there?" Frank had. It was large, grander than most he'd seen while he had travelled through France. "It was mine, or due to be mine. I married an octogenarian. Yes, it was like necrophilia, if that's what you're thinking."

"I wasn't thinking any such thing."

"Anyway, he died yesterday. His son turned up this morning waving the will at me. He'd persuaded the old devil to change it. He'd cut me out completely. His son threw me out of the place and took the car keys. So I'm on my way to town to get some cash before he takes me off the bank account, and to buy some valuables I can resell before he does the same with the credit cards.

"You probably think that I'm being dishonest, but you didn't have to live with the old man for three years. He smelt of Camembert most of the time. Don't get me wrong, I love cheese but I don't want the aroma twenty-four hours a day.

"And as for his son, he never bothered with his father, never did anything for him. Just poisoned him against me. I tell you what, I'll buy you dinner. And I'll get you a room in the best hotel in town. I may as well spend his money while I still can, I've certainly earned it. What do you say?"

"I don't know."

"Well, if you prefer to sleep in this tin can."

"No, you're right. It would make a nice change. Thank you."

Frank luxuriated in the bath in his room at the Hotel du Roi while Delphine was out shopping. A good soak was one thing he'd really missed these past few months, and he'd never been in a bathroom like this before. The bath was deep and spacious with taps of gold and had four feet shaped like lion's paws. Definitely a cut above the small avocado-coloured one at home he'd installed back in the seventies.

It was good to feel warmed right through. The nights were chilly now. In Brunhild, he had started going to bed wearing his clothes.

Meeting Delphine down in the lobby an hour later as arranged, she presented him with some bags. He gave her a quizzical look.

"For you. Some clothes."

"Why?"

"Because you're about to eat at the best restaurant in the region, not McDonalds."

With a huff, Frank returned to his room and changed into the shirt and jacket she had purchased. The jacket didn't bother him, it was blue. The shirt he was less comfortable with, pink like Brunhild had once been. But this was France, and the men here didn't seem hung up on things like that.

Frank discovered eating in France was a very different experience to Germany and what he was used to in England. The presentation was an art form in itself and the flavours sublime.

Frank considered the quantities small until he found out that the courses kept on coming. Despite a lifetime of no gastronomic exploration of any kind, he was surprisingly enamoured with it all as well as the wines Delphine ordered. His mouth was on a delicious voyage of discovery.

While they ate, he had time to observe her in detail. Probably in her mid fifties, she was wearing a new dress and enough jewellery to keep her in comfort for some considerable time should she need to sell it.

Her chestnut hair, no longer flattened to her scalp, she had put up in an elegant bun. Frank wondered if Delphine was a ballet dancer when younger. He was fascinated by her hands, long delicate fingers ending in carefully manicured nails painted red like those of a diva. If not a ballet dancer, he bet that she must have been a singer or an actress. She was without doubt the most exotic person he had ever met.

Frank couldn't work her out. Her mahogany eyes were unfathomable. When she spoke she became animated and they seemed to sparkle, but when not talking there was something wistful about her.

"Where did you learn to speak such good English?" asked Frank.

"Through my job."

"A lot of international travel?"

"Yes."

"What did you do? No, let me guess. Something in entertainment."

"You could put it that way. I was an escort for the rich and famous."

Frank nearly choked on his coquilles Saint Jacques.

"Are you shocked?"

"A little surprised. You ... you don't look like one."

Delphine laughed. "We come in all guises. We're ordinary humans like everyone else."

"What about your husband?"

"An old client. I was able to give it up when I married him. Or thought I had until now. So now you know my secrets, what about yours, Frank?"

"Nothing so exciting. Recently retired and seeing death looming on the horizon, I was bored. In a rut. So I decided to go abroad. For the very first time."

"Are you enjoying it?"

"Yes, it's sort of liberating. No responsibilities and no norms to conform to."

"When did you start?"

"The end of summer. I went to Germany first. I'm heading to Spain for a few weeks until the money runs out and I have to go home."

"Do you want to go home?"

"I did initially, though not anymore. I'm enjoying seeing new places. But I can't afford to travel much longer."

Delphine lit a cigarette and exhaled, a glint in her eyes. "We should become partners then."

Frank couldn't hide his astonishment. "Me, a pimp? I don't think so."

"No, that's not what I have in mind. Those days are over for me. Look, I know where to go to mingle with the wealthy. I could distract them while you take their valuables."

"Become a thief?"

"I prefer to think of it as wealth redistribution. I expect you worked hard all your life for not very much, no?"

"You can say that again."

"These people we would target, most of them have never done a day's work in their lives. They inherited it all. And they have so much, they wouldn't miss the odd trinket. You wouldn't believe how much they own. More than some countries. What do you think?"

"The answer's no."

"What a shame. We would have made a good team you and I. Here's to a missed opportunity." Delphine raised her glass. "À votre santé."

Frank didn't sleep well that night. All that food and wine. And thinking of his evening with Delphine kept him awake too. But it didn't matter. Travel most certainly wasn't dull. You encountered such interesting characters along the way.

While he sat eating breakfast in a corner of the dining room the next day, she appeared.

"Good morning, Frank. Do you mind if I join you?"

"No, of course not."

"I thought maybe after last night, you wouldn't want to be seen with me."

"Not at all."

Delphine poured herself a coffee from the pot the waiter had brought. "We have a slight problem. When I went to pay this morning, my cards wouldn't work. Obviously, Philippe has already cancelled them. I need to hang on to the cash I've got. I don't know how long it's going to have to last. We'll need to do a runner as you English say."

"I have some money. How much is the bill?"

"Six thousand Francs."

"What! That's like six hundred pounds."

"Quality costs."

"Well, I can't afford that. It'd just about clear me out."

"No need to worry. Get your things and wait for me out front in the van in ten minutes time."

"But-"

DAVID CANFORD

"We don't have a choice."

CHAPTER 12

Frank was nervously tapping his fingers on the steering wheel when Delphine emerged from the side of the hotel, pulling the Louis Vuitton suitcase she'd bought the day before. As he helped her into the camper van with it, they heard shouting. The man from reception stood at the top of the steps by the front entrance, gesticulating, his face a cauldron of anger.

"Let's go. Hurry."

Frank needed no second bidding.

"Oh, that was fun," laughed Delphine once they'd made their getaway.

"Fun? Not exactly what I'd call it."

"Do lighten up, Frank. See what a good duo we'd make."

"Until the police caught us."

"They wouldn't. Have you always been so old even when you were young?"

Frank didn't reply but he knew the answer.

"Follow that sign for la Gare and take me to the station. I'm going to catch a train to Nice. If you change your mind, I'll be staying at the Hotel Le

Negresco. It's opposite the sea and the Promenade des Anglais. You can't miss it."

"But you have no credit cards that work."

"I'll find a way, I always do. Life isn't for the faint-hearted."

Arriving at the railway station, she pecked him on the cheek before getting out.

"Thanks for everything. Au revoir, my strange Englishman."

Frank experienced a pang of regret when he drove off. Delphine was good company. Still, a life of crime probably wasn't the best idea at his age.

He didn't stop until the afternoon, wanting to make sure he had put a long distance between him and the hotel. According to his atlas, he wasn't far from the coast, somewhere north of Montpellier. With luck, he'd reach the Spanish border later today.

But his luck ran out. Brunhild spluttered more loudly than ever when he tried to start her again and then became silent. Having recently driven through a small town, Frank walked back along the road to find a garage.

"My car is broken. Kaput," he said to the garage mechanic emerging in oil-stained blue overalls from under the chassis of the car he was working on. "Down the road." Frank pointed in the direction from which he'd come.

"Venez avec moi," said the man. Frank didn't understand until the man walked outside and jumped into the recovery truck parked out front.

GOING BIG OR SMALL?

Frank did understand the sucking sound the mechanic made after inspecting Brunhild's engine,.

"How much?"

The man pulled a notebook and a biro from the pocket of his overalls. He tore off the page he'd written on with a flourish and presented it to Frank.

"Nine thousand francs!" exclaimed Frank.

The mechanic responded with the characteristic Gallic shrug. Take it or leave it, I don't care was the message.

"That's as much as she cost to buy."

The man shrugged again, it wasn't his problem. Frank was without a choice.

"Okay."

The man attached a line which he activated to pull the van up a ramp onto the flatbed truck. Back at the garage, he beckoned his assistant.

"My boss says five days."

"Five days?"

"He has to order the parts. The car is rare and he needs money before he buys them. Five thousand now please."

"I don't have that much on me. Is there a bank nearby?"

"Yes, over there by the patisserie."

When he returned with the money, Frank asked where he could stay.

"Hotel de la Poste. It's the only one there is."

It was a modest establishment but then Frank

wasn't used to fancy places, or any at all for that matter. He could count the number of nights in his life he'd spent in a hotel on the fingers of one hand. The bathroom was a revelation, but not in a nice way like the previous night's hotel. It was very French. The toilet was unlike one Frank had ever seen. He remembered Gayle telling him about them from her visits with Morris. It was like a shower tray with raised footprints and a hole at the back.

Frank wet his shoes the first time he pressed the flush. To his disgust, the water flooded the footprints which he was still standing upon. He didn't understand that the sign 'Appuyez doucement' meant press gently. What surprised him even more was that the toilet doubled as a shower, with a shower head above it. Why on earth would anyone combine a toilet and a shower, he muttered to himself.

Five days in a small French town when you don't speak the language, and the wet winter weather keeps you confined indoors for most of the time, seemed like an eternity to Frank. There wasn't a lot to see. A church and a war memorial was the extent of it. But then it was a whole lot better than the weeks locked in his cell which he'd experienced in East Berlin.

Visiting the town's bookshop, Frank found a teach yourself English book and bought it. What he failed to appreciate until he got the book back to his room at the hotel was that although he could read the English phrases and see their French equivalents, he didn't have a clue how to pronounce them.

Frank became a fixture at the cafe beneath the hotel where several of the local men gathered late each morning for a glass of red wine. The cafe smelled of Gauloises cigarettes and the garlic on their breath from their previous night's dinner. One of them spoke good English.

"I was in England during the war, part of the Free French. We still think you abandoned us at Dunkirk. You left us all alone, instead of staying to fight the Germans. Probably one of the reasons De Gaulle kept saying 'non' when you wanted to join the EU. And now you're in it, all you do is moan and try to stop every new idea we come up with."

"I'd never thought of it that way," said Frank.

"My mother used to say 'Always piss towards the North because that's where the English are.' But having lived amongst you, I understand how you feel. La Manche, that little sea between us, is like your moat. It keeps you safe and makes you feel separate. For us, there is no such safety or separateness. The Germans came marching into France three times in less than a hundred years. That's why we understand how important it is to be linked together, to make war impossible. Anyway, cheers my friend."

"Santé," responded Frank, who was proud he could now say 'cheers' in three languages. He clinked glasses with all five men sitting around the table.

"What do you think of your Mrs Thatcher?"

"She's a controversial figure, you either love her or hate her. Around us lots of the coal mines and factories have closed since she took over so she's not very popular."

"We wouldn't let that happen in France. When the government tries to close something or interfere with our welfare benefits, we take to the streets. The farmers block the roads, burn a few tyres, and the government backs down. It always works. We're very protective of our lifestyle. We don't want to end up like the Americans, working sixty hours a week with no job protection, and eating processed food which tastes of nothing."

"I'd have to agree with you there."

"A country should be run for its people, not big business. Liberté, egalité, fraternité. It comes from our revolution."

When not in the cafe or sleeping, Frank spent a lot of time thinking. He would have to go home now given the cost of Brunhild's repairs. He'd never get to see Spain or spend a winter somewhere warm. Turning the pages of his atlas, Frank looked at the roads and place names which he would never get to visit, moving his finger across the page on his imaginary journey while he did so.

It didn't seem fair. He'd never had much and had never taken much, but you couldn't spend what you didn't have. His adventure was finished. Back to old Blighty to wait out his days.

Finally, Brunhild was ready. She drove like new,

well like a new Barkas that is, a tortoise not a hare. His new friends from the cafe came out to wave him off. He did baulk slightly at being kissed on both cheeks. How his acquaintances at the Queen Mary would tease him if they could see him now.

Within a mile, Frank's goodbye smile and happiness at getting a send-off had evaporated. He didn't want to go home. Life had been so interesting these last few months. He'd seen so much and learned so much. Even his time in jail in East Berlin held a certain frisson of excitement for him looking back on it.

Wealth redistribution, Delphine called it. Would it really be so bad? After all, he could no longer claim to be a law-abiding citizen. He'd absconded from the police in Germany and ignored a parking fine in Strasbourg as well as illegally crossing a border. And he'd left the hotel where he and Delphine stayed without paying.

Maybe she was right. Would those they took it from really miss it? Didn't they already have enough, more than their fair share?

But he'd be breaking the law. But whose laws? Laws that protected the wealthy. And hadn't they also stolen, stolen from people like him? Getting rich on the backs of him and millions like him by paying paltry wages to make huge profits?

His own boss had run the company which Frank worked for into the ground. Asset stripping the receiver called it. Selling off what the company owned to raise the money for that Yuppie from

London to pay off the loan the company then guaranteed so that he could buy it in the first place. That young man from Chelsea had ended up owning something which he'd never paid for and never had any intention of doing so. To Frank, that seemed like theft on a grand scale.

The man only ever came up North once to look at the factory. In the end, there wasn't enough money left to pay Frank and the other workers the company pension they'd paid into for years. Yet the bastard was living in the Bahamas with a mansion and a big yacht. He'd never been held accountable, and never would be. There was one set of rules for those at the top, another for everybody else. If you could afford accountants and lawyers, you could get away with all sorts of shenanigans.

I wouldn't need much, reasoned Frank. Only enough for campsites and some food. I could give the rest away to the poor. A modern day Robin Hood. No, it was a silly fantasy. Get a grip and act your age, man.

He reached a crossroads. Right was north and England, left south and the Mediterranean. Frank turned right.

CHAPTER 13

Regretting his decision only a few miles later, Frank applied the brakes suddenly, spun around, and went southeast towards Marseille. It was time to stop finding reasons not to do something, he told himself. Time to just bloody well do it.

Nice wasn't far from Marseille. Frank had seen it in his atlas. What harm could there be going to find out a bit more about Delphine's plan? He could always leave if he changed his mind.

Marseille was a traffic nightmare. Frank got lost. He missed the bypass and ended up in the city centre. Cars crisscrossed in all directions, communicating by non-stop blasts on the horn.

Frank had a couple of near misses. He became familiar with the raised forearm and fist and a slap on that arm just above the right angle next to the elbow with the hand of the other arm. It was clearly the same greeting as two fingers back home.

"It might be safer if you kept both hands on the wheel," shouted Frank, but those concerned were long gone by then, and most probably wouldn't have understood even if they'd heard him. He enjoyed a good rant when on four wheels. Safe in his little metal box, he would say things he would never have dreamed of saying if someone in the street bumped into him. Gayle often used to tell him he'd end up getting punched one day.

Once out of the city and pootling along the coast road, he relaxed again. Despite it being December, there was a lustrous quality to the light in this part of the world which refreshed him. He could see why royalty and film stars were attracted to the south of France.

When he reached Nice, the Hotel Le Negresco was easy to find like Delphine said it would be. A magnificent building of bright white with a tiled roof of salmon pink, it stood out prominently from its surroundings. The hotel's frontage was reminiscent of a cross between a French chateau and a plantation mansion from the Deep South with a rounded tower crowned by a bulbous top at one end. It was without doubt a unique and striking building.

Frank went a few streets back to park Brunhild, and changed into the clothes which Delphine had given him. The hotel looked the kind of place where people would dress up, and he didn't want to draw attention to himself by being the odd one out.

The interior was even more eclectic than the exterior. Beyond the reception, four large stands in gold and black held golden candelabra lights, beckoning him beyond to Roman columns leading into a massive room with a glazed roof reminiscent of a pavilion at Kew Gardens.

From the ceiling hung enormous chandeliers. Guests sat on reproduction French chairs. Various sculptures adorned the massive space and works of art decorated the walls. Frank had never seen anything quite like it.

He scanned those sitting there but couldn't see Delphine so he retreated into the bar of dark wood by reception, ordering only a small bottle of water. Memories of the size of the bill at the Hotel du Roi were still fresh in his mind.

Not sure what to do next, he wandered outside and crossed the six-lane road divided in the middle by palm trees and onto the wide promenade above the pebble beach. The Promenade des Anglais was funded by members of the local Anglican Church, who under the guidance of their vicar had it constructed to give work to beggars in the 1820s. In those days, British aristocrats used to flock to Nice to escape the cold winter at home.

It was said that even Queen Victoria shed her dourness, becoming girlish and exuberant when visiting Nice which she did several times in the sunset of her reign. On her deathbed, she is reputed to have said, "Oh, if only I were at Nice, I should recover."

Frank too experienced the restorative effects of the Mediterranean air while he strolled westwards besides the Baie des Anges, the Bay of Angels.

Delphine was right. Life was for the taking. If you waited to be asked, you'd miss out.

The thought of home no longer exerted any pull. If he never went back, he doubted he would regret it. He had a new life now, a much more exciting and fulfilling one.

Entering the hotel again, Frank saw Delphine walking into the bar, dressed in an evening gown. He hurried after her.

Too late. She was already sitting next to a man in a dinner jacket of a similar age, running her fingers playfully through her hair and tossing her head back in laughter. Frank was about to retreat when the man got up and went over to the bar. Frank seized the opportunity.

"Delphine, it's me, Frank."

"Frank? I never expected to see you again."

"Me neither. I've changed my mind. If you still want to that is."

"Of course I do. I'll get his key. Then I'll pretend I've left something in my room and go up there. It's room 305. Follow me up. Go sit over there, he'll be back any second."

From a corner of the bar, Frank watched Delphine at work. She put her arms around the man and kissed him playfully. Expertly she felt the side of his jacket, one hand sliding into the pocket and finding the key, which she dropped into the clutch bag beside her. Job done, she said something to him and left. Frank followed at a discreet distance.

"We can say hello properly now," said Delphine

opening her door when he knocked. She leant forwards offering one cheek and then the other for the traditional French greeting.

"I'm so glad you've decided to join me, operating alone isn't easy. We're off to the Opéra for the evening. I'll let you into his room. Take whatever you find is worthwhile, and meet me tomorrow morning at ten at the Café Flaubert in Place Massena in the centre of town."

"What if he's put everything in the room safe?"

"Stay there and hide in the cupboard when he gets back. He's wearing an expensive Rolex. I'm sure he'll take it off when he gets into bed, and I doubt he'll put it in the safe overnight."

"That sounds risky."

"Life is a risk."

"Will you be er..." Frank searched for an innocuous way of describing what he imagined would be happening later, "distracting him?"

"No, I'll be back in my room, sleeping. If I came to his room, he'd suspect me tomorrow when he finds something missing. This way he'll have no clue who it was. Come, he's on the floor below."

Each floor of the hotel was decorated with a different theme. Delphine's floor was French imperial with a portrait of Napoleon and others from that epoch. This next floor was African-themed with sculptures from that continent and a big picture of a smiling Louis Armstrong. The black and white striped carpet was like a zebra's markings.

"Good luck. See you tomorrow," said Delphine pushing Frank through the man's bedroom door.

"But-"

CHAPTER 14

It was too late to object. Delphine had already shut Frank in the room and left.

Frank was struck by how grand the room was. A large bed with a golden painted-headboard, scenes of ancient China for wallpaper, armchairs, a desk, gilded mirrors, and a balcony looking out to sea.

So this was how the other half lived. Though it wasn't half, it was only a privileged few. Frank bet that the occupant had never laid awake at night worrying about how he was going to pay for his children's school uniforms, or had needed to borrow money from loan sharks to bail out his son for drug dealing.

He began to look around for something worth taking. There was some money on the desk table. Frank counted it. Less than a thousand francs. Looking in drawers and cupboards, he found nothing which appeared to have much value.

Frank wanted to leave. Hiding and waiting until the man returned and fell asleep filled Frank with the apprehension of discovery, of being arrested and thrown in jail. But then if he'd taken nothing, what could they do? Anyway, he could just run out and away. Such thoughts gave him Dutch courage, for a while.

He scouted for a place to hide. The bathroom wouldn't work, the man would almost certainly go in there on his return. Likewise, he would probably open the cupboard to hang up his jacket. There was the balcony, but he might lock the door to that before going to bed. Under the bed seemed the only option.

Frank tried it out for size, making old people moans and grunts while he manoeuvred his inflexible body into the narrow gap between the floor and the bed. He would need to remember to suppress those involuntary noises. They came so naturally now, he was usually no longer aware he was making them.

It was funny how old age stole a march on you that way. All those things which he had noticed about his parents and made fun of, he was doubtless doing himself without realising. Never mock the old, he thought. It would come back and bite you on the backside much sooner than you ever expected.

Realising that lying under the bed for any length of time would be too uncomfortable, Frank slithered back out in an ungainly manner and sat in an armchair. It was only seven. He couldn't imagine they'd be back before eleven.

Frank awoke with a jolt. A key was turning in the lock. He would never have time to get across the room and under the bed. He panicked. What should he do? Push past him and run? The curtains. Yes! He leapt out of the chair and hid behind them.

His heart beating like a drum, Frank listened as the man pottered about the room while getting ready for bed, releasing an evening's worth of retained farts in the process. Frank was only just out of sight behind the undrawn curtains. He prayed that if the man closed them he wouldn't look to his side and spot the intruder.

In the event, he went to bed with them open. The moon cast a pale light into the room. Frank waited for what seemed like an age until he heard snoring. Leaving his textile sanctuary, he advanced towards the bed.

He could see the watch lying on the bedside table. Gingerly, he put his hand out for it. It was heavy compared to any watch he'd ever owned.

The man suddenly sat up bolt right in bed. Frank froze with terror as if glued to the spot.

The man began shouting. Frank was about to drop the watch and run until he noticed the man wasn't looking at him. The man flopped back down on the pillow.

Frank swallowed as his tension dropped from acute to severe. Someone else who talked in their sleep like him.

Intent on making no noise, Frank crept carefully backwards until he reached the door. As nonchalantly as he could with legs that felt like jelly, Frank descended the staircase and walked past the big Christmas tree in reception and into the night.

The following morning, he went to Place Masséna, a huge square on the edge of the old town enclosed by neoclassical buildings painted in red and dark pink. Frank made his way along under the colonnaded walkways to the cafe. Every few steps he patted his pocket to confirm that the Rolex was still there, anxious that he might have his pockets picked by a thief.

"Superbe," enthused Delphine when she took the iconic timepiece from him while they indulged in hot chocolate and warm beignets. The small fried doughnuts were yet another culinary delight she introduced Frank to. "I should be able to get well over fifty thousand francs for this. We shall have ourselves a Christmas to remember."

"Did you see him this morning?"

"Yes, he thinks it was an inside job. One of the staff."

"Did you tell him you were leaving?"

"I said there was a family emergency, and I had to return to Paris. Anyway, I think he'd already lost interest when I refused his invitation for a nightcap back in his room. Can you meet me back here at three. We'll go to Menton. It's a beautiful town on the Italian border with the best climate in all of France, famous for its lemons."

That afternoon Delphine's smile was broader than usual.

"Seventy thousand francs. That's thirty-five thousand each. Not bad for a few hours work, is it?"

Three and a half thousand pounds. Who said crime didn't pay? It was considerably more than Frank's annual pension. In the divorce settlement, Gayle got a large chunk of his pension, and after she'd married Morris, Frank never went back to court to get that changed. He'd been worried the lawyers would charge him so much he would have been in debt for years until the extra pension covered their fee. Gayle had insisted they use lawyers when they got divorced to make sure it was done properly and he'd never forgotten the thousands which that cost.

Menton was charming. Old five-storey buildings painted in yellow or rose pink, orange or saffron, with shutters of turquoise climbed its hill. Festive lights hung above the steep and narrow alleyways. "You should see the place in February when they have the lemon festival. They create fantastic sculptures out of oranges and lemons. Pyramids, a Taj Mahal, elephants, even whales. It's a wonderful sight. A carnival to mark the end of winter. Not that they have much of one here."

Delphine took a room in a hotel. Frank chose to stay in Brunhild.

The next morning, he wandered around the old town, climbing to the cemetery at the top where the great and good were buried. English, Russians and Germans were among them. They had sought to improve their health by coming here, without much success it appeared, working out their ages from the dates of death on the headstones. The dead had stupendous views looking across the bay, and behind rose mountains now covered in snow.

"What a waste, they can't see a bloody thing," muttered Frank before beginning his descent to meet up with Delphine.

"As it's Christmas Eve today, I've booked us a traditional dinner, the Reveillon. Many have it after midnight mass."

"I'd have indigestion if I ate that late," said Frank.

"I thought you might say that so we're starting at seven. That way we'll be finished in time for mass."

"It takes that long?"

"We French take our time eating. It's for pleasure, not an inhalation like a dog."

"Can I have turkey?"

"Of course. After the oysters and foie gras and before the cheese and dessert, all washed down with champagne."

A few weeks ago Frank wouldn't have tried anything but meat and two veg. That evening he enjoyed every course, a man transformed.

"You don't have to accompany me to church. There's an Anglican one here if you prefer, even a Russian Orthodox," said Delphine.

"I never go to church, except for weddings and funerals. I'll give it a miss thanks. I'll walk you there and then head back to Brunhild."

The basilica with its campanile, or bell tower,

stood high above the bay welcoming a long stream of people with its floodlit exterior. Frank escorted Delphine to the door as the bells were striking midnight. Even though he wasn't going in, he could understand the attraction. It was so atmospheric on a night like this.

"Merry Christmas, Delphine."

"Joyeux Noel, Frank."

Returning towards Brunhild, Frank noticed a young man bedding down on cardboard in a shop doorway.

"Happy Christmas," said Frank giving him a large wad of curled up notes from his pocket.

CHAPTER 15

"We should go to Monte Carlo for New Year," said Delphine while they sat in bright sunshine one morning drinking coffee at a cafe near the port and looking out on a flat calm sea of aquamarine. "And go gambling at the casino."

"I've never been a gambling man."

"You really haven't had much fun, have you Frank? You'll enjoy it. Besides, it's a fertile hunting ground."

"So long as I don't have to hide in someone's bedroom again."

"You won't but you'll need a dinner jacket and a dress shirt. And new shoes. You'd stand out a mile in those scruffy boots. We'll visit Nice first, things are much more expensive in Monaco."

Monaco was like a Mediterranean Manhattan or European Hong Kong. Hemmed in by mountains, this tiny kingdom of less than one square mile lacks space. There had been no choice but to build upwards. Lights from numerous high-rise apartment blocks peppered the night sky when they arrived.

Frank felt conspicuous as he parked Brunhild. She had always stood out to some extent, her unusual looks often attracting comment, but here she looked like Cinderella unable to go to the ball. All around her were Ferraris, Rolls Royces, and Lamborghinis.

"How can people afford these cars?" asked Frank.

"Because they don't pay tax. While the likes of you were paying it, those with a million times more were paying nothing. Tax exiles. So if we get anything tonight, there's no need to feel guilty. You know, Frank, I'm surprised you're not a Catholic."

"Why?"

"Because we're brought up to think that pleasure and extravagance are a sin, just like you."

"Maybe the communists were right," said Frank.

"What, make everyone equally poor and miserable? The rich can easily move somewhere else. I prefer to join them, and take a little piece for myself. Now grab your passport and let's go. You'll need to bring it with you because for some strange reason the citizens of Monaco can't enter the gambling room, so they check everyone who does to confirm they're a foreigner."

The casino was an imposing building from La Belle Époque. Frank hesitated when he glimpsed the glamorous throng of people entering. He felt like a duck out of water.

The poshest event that he'd ever been to was his firm's one hundredth anniversary celebration at the Railway Hotel several years ago. That had been dowdy by comparison which ended in a drunken brawl. Frank ended the evening with a broken nose when Gayle told Majorie Dawes that Majorie's husband was having an affair with Sylvia Jones, and Sylvia's husband had mistakenly thought Frank was Tony Dawes.

Sensing Frank's unease, Delphine sought to bolster his confidence.

"You look so handsome this evening. Doesn't it feel good to be dressed up and going to a party?"

"I suppose it does."

"Come on then, double-O-seven."

"His grandfather, maybe."

Inside, it was a scene of chandeliers and large mirrors. The place was humming; everyone crammed shoulder to shoulder, ladies dripping with jewellery and in designer dresses. Frank smacked his lips together, the air tasted of perfume and aftershave.

"Blimey, that looks like Michael Cain over there," said Frank.

"Well, it most probably is. You get a lot of famous people here."

Waiters skilfully negotiated the crowds with trays of champagne and canapés.

"Let's go try our luck in La Salle des Jeux," said Delphine.

"The what?"

"The games room."

"You're right, it is like a James Bond film," said Frank.

"Do you fancy your luck on the roulette wheel?"
"I don't know how to play."
"It's not difficult. You buy some tokens, and place them on the numbers you think will win."
"A thousand francs then."
"Where's the thrill in that? You won't get excited unless it really makes a difference. I say ten thousand."
"But that's most of what I've got left," protested Frank.
"So what. Just give it to me. We can get more where that came from. And if you win, you make thirty-six times what you bet."
"Aren't there any less risky odds than that?"
"Yes, you double your money if you choose red or black and win, but you'll never win big that way. Here, have some more champagne and loosen up."
Delphine grabbed two glasses as a waiter passed by. Reluctantly, Frank gave her his money and downed the champagne in one.
"Here you go. Your tokens," said Delphine returning a few moments later.
"Where's yours?"
"I'm not playing. I won't have beginner's luck like you. Which number do you want to bet on?"
"I'll start with sixteen. A thousand Francs a time."
"Okay, you win," sighed Delphine.
While he put the tokens down, Frank could hardly believe what he was doing. He doubted even Gayle and Morris would place bets that big with so little chance of winning.

The croupier spun the wheel. Mesmerised, Frank watched the ball, hands clutched together protectively in front of him as if he were back at the nudist camp again.

The wheel slowed, the ball dropped into position. There was the silence of anticipation from those crowded around the table.

"Numero seize," announced the croupier.

Frank leaned forward to see where it had landed.

"Sixteen?"

"Yes. What a waste," said Delphine.

The croupier pushed a mass of tokens towards Frank, almost more than he could pick up.

"I hardly think so."

Frank had never won so much money in his life.

"You could have won three hundred and sixty thousand francs not only thirty-six thousand if you'd trusted me. I'm going to circulate and see who's here. I'll be back later."

Frank stayed at the table, gradually losing all his winnings. Afterwards, he wandered around aimlessly, morose at his losses until Delphine took him by the arm.

"Quick, we must go outside. It's nearly midnight."

The crowd outside were shouting the countdown. Immediately after "un", there were loud bangs and fireworks turned the sky into fountains of white.

"Bonne année, Frank. It's 1990! A new decade."

Delphine kissed him on the lips. Frank kissed her back but she pulled away.

"I have to go now, I've been invited to a party on a

yacht. I expect it will last all night. I'll be back at your van as soon as I can."

Frank watched her go. She waved at a man emerging from the casino and walked with him to the door of a Rolls Royce which the chauffeur was holding open for them.

Frank's shoulders slumped, the promise of her New Year's kiss gone. She was like a butterfly, mesmerising but impossible to catch. Snap out of it, he told himself, this was only ever a business arrangement. Nothing more. Why would she ever fancy an old fart like you?

A gentle tapping on the glass of Brunhild at about 5am woke him. Pulling back the curtains, he saw Delphine waving excitedly. He got up to let her in.

"Good party?"

"Not really, but never mind about that. I met an art dealer. He lives in a villa in the hills behind Cannes, and he's leaving for Paris this morning."

"I'm not following you."

"Why don't you drive us back into France. We'll find a hotel, get washed and changed and I'll explain."

CHAPTER 16

"Just because he's not there, doesn't mean you can walk in and take his best painting. Even if he lives alone, there'll be an alarm," said Frank after Delphine had told him her plan.

"His housekeeper will be there."

"Exactly. We can't take it from under her nose."

"That's because you have no imagination, Frank. We'll need to hire a Mercedes. You won't look like my chauffeur if I arrive in this old tin can. And we have some shopping to do."

The villa was situated back from the road down a gravel driveway that made a pleasing sound as the tyres crunched over it, although Frank was far too anxious to pay any attention to that.

In his recently acquired grey uniform and peaked cap, he followed Delphine up the steps to the entrance holding a large rectangular package wrapped in brown paper. Delphine was dressed in black with a thin veil hanging from her hat. The grieving widow come to get a valuation.

The housekeeper opened one of the two tall double doors in response to the knock on the large brass knocker in the shape of a lion's head.

Although Frank couldn't understand the conversation, he had been briefed. Delphine would be explaining she'd travelled hours to get here, not knowing Monsieur would be away. She was certain he'd said he would be available to see her. Would it be possible to at least come in and take a coffee? Her driver too if Madame didn't mind.

They were invited into the living room. It was furnished in Louis XVI style with several large paintings adorning the walls.

"I would say that one," said Delphine pointing at a pastoral scene of vibrant colours in Impressionist style. "It's like one my husband had. It must be the same artist. He always said it was extremely valuable."

Hearing the door open, she quickly sat down in a chair, feigning exhaustion.

Once the coffee had been delivered, Delphine asked Frank to lift down the painting.

"What if it's alarmed?"

"I hardly think he would alarm each painting. Look how many are here in this one room alone."

It was heavier than expected and Frank dropped it. A loud thump echoed when the frame hit the floor. Delphine scowled at him. They waited with bated breath but the housekeeper didn't reappear.

Delphine unwrapped the painting which she had purchased earlier that day for a mere five hundred Francs and then began wrapping up the one they were taking in the same brown paper.

"Hang up the one I brought," she commanded. "The housekeeper probably won't even notice the change. The frame and size are very similar as well as the style. I chose well."

Frank stood on tiptoes to reach the hook.

"Don't drop it this time."

"Merci beaucoup, Madame," she called down the corridor as they left. The housekeeper appeared from a door at the far end and raised a hand.

"Au revoir, Madame."

"It's such a relief to get this stupid hat off," said Delphine from the back of the car as they sped away. "I think the chauffeur's uniform suits you though, especially the cap."

Frank wasn't listening, he was looking in his rear mirror expecting to see flashing blue lights. Yet he was also enjoying the adrenaline rush from their excursion. Delphine was right, stealing was much easier than he'd thought it would be and strangely satisfying.

"I'll take the painting to an art dealer in Nice tomorrow. Then we'll plan our next move."

"Well?" asked Frank when he arrived at the table in the Café Flaubert where Delphine was waiting the following afternoon.

"Five thousand francs."

"Not such a good choice then."

"It's a fake. The dealer showed me how to spot it."

"That's that then," said Frank in an 'I told you so' tone.

"No, it gives us an even better opportunity."

"How?"

"I'd say the art dealer is a fraudster, peddling fake artworks to his customers."

"So what if he is?"

"Because we can make more money out of that than we ever could from one painting. We'll call him on it. If he's not defrauding people, he won't be concerned. But if he is, he'll be willing to pay big time to keep that a secret."

"You mean blackmail him?" Frank's voice trembled at the idea.

"I prefer to think of it as sharing the proceeds of his business."

"I'm not sure about this. Blackmail's a whole new ball game."

"Why? I thought it would appeal to your conscience more. We wouldn't be stealing from someone who might be considered innocent. He appears to be a crook. How can taking money from a criminal be wrong?"

"Well, I suppose so. How will you do it?"

"Me? I can't. He already knows what I sound like and look like."

Frank leaned back in his chair, his arms crossed in refusal.

"You've got to be joking. I'm not doing it. He might shoot me."

"Over the telephone? I don't think so. I'll tell you what you need to say. He speaks excellent English."

"I won't ever have to meet him?"

"No. That tends to be the way it works. You're not

planning on becoming his best friend."
"Hmm."
"Why do you British always talk in code? All this "Hmm" and "Mmm". What do they mean? A good way of avoiding answering the question, in my opinion. Garçon," called Delphine catching the attention of a waiter. "Un cognac pour Monsieur. Un grand. I'm getting you a large brandy."
Later in a public phone box, Frank made the call with Delphine whispering into his ear whenever he floundered.
"Allo, Gustave Beauchamp."
"Mr. Beauchamp, I'm aware of the fact that you're selling fake paintings and pocketing the proceeds."
"Who is this? I don't know what you're talking about. You're crazy."
The line went dead.
"He's hung up."
"Well, ring again," insisted Delphine. "That tactic isn't going to work."
Frank did as ordered.
"Putting the phone down won't work, Mr. Beauchamp, not unless you want the police to know."
"What is it that you want?"
There was an unmistakeable concern in his voice. Delphine's instinct was correct.
"A million francs."
"You must be out of your mind."
"Okay then, I'll go to the police."
The response was quick.

"No, that won't be necessary. But it'll take me a few days to raise that much."

"Good, now you're seeing sense."

Frank was ad-libbing, getting into the part and beginning to enjoy himself as if he were in some Hollywood gangster film. Delphine glared at him to stay on script.

"I want it in used notes. In a briefcase. Leave it behind the statue of the Virgin Mary on the mountain road. Have it there by noon on Wednesday. And don't try and play any games. No one is to be anywhere near the pick up point."

"Are you the man who stole the painting while I was away, turning up with some woman claiming she needed my expert opinion?"

"I don't know what you're talking about. It sounds like you have more than one problem. Remember, by noon Wednesday."

Delphine cut the line.

"I hadn't finished," protested Frank.

"That was perfect. You said all that was needed."

Frank was pleased with himself. "It was so easy. I should've done this years ago."

"Well, it's never too late. You're doing it now. Anyway, if you'd done it on your own, you'd be in jail or dead."

"Thanks a lot."

"Come on Frank, you're hardly Al Capone."

Frank's elation that the call had worked had given way to collywobbles come Wednesday, a feeling compounded by having to steer Brunhild up the steep and narrow twisting road. The coast and the Mediterranean were far below.

"Drive past so we can check there's nobody about," ordered Delphine when they reached the spot.

The Virgin was about three foot high on a pedestal, her arms and hands raised as though imploring them not to do this. No one was in evidence, so Frank turned Brunhild around in a farm track and headed back towards the Virgin. A woman was now there placing some flowers and saying a prayer.

"Pull over. She'll be gone in a minute."

And she was, giving them a quizzical look as she passed by.

Frank climbed out and looked behind the statue. There it was. A brown briefcase. Back in the van, Delphine opened it and briefly examined the contents.

"It looks like it's all here. We can go."

They began to round the first of the many tight bends which would get them back to town.

Frank swallowed hard. "I think we're being followed."

Delphine turned her head. A black Mercedes was gaining on them.

"No, it's just someone in a hurry. Let them-"

She never got to finish her sentence. She screamed when the back window shattered from the impact of bullets.

CHAPTER 17

Accelerating, Frank took the next corner too fast. He lost control and Brunhild veered off the road and into a precipitously sloping field.

Frantically he swung the wheel first one way and then the other, trying to avoid oncoming olive trees. Their branches shattered the windscreen. All the while Brunhild shuddered violently as if she was going to break into pieces at any moment. Twice she took to the air. Although he was probably hurtling towards death, Frank surprised himself and didn't panic. With grim determination, he kept focused.

An encounter with a tree somehow ripped the passenger door off. The briefcase fell from Delphine's lap, opening as it went flying. Bank notes in their hundreds fluttered like feathers. Brunhild toppled and rolled over before finally coming to a halt lying on her right side.

"Are you all right?" asked Frank.

"Yes, I think so. Let's get out."

Frank climbed out and leaned back in to offer Delphine, who had now undone her seat belt, a helping hand.

"Bloody hell. That was a close run thing."

"It might not be over yet. Grab as many notes as you can."

Delphine was already chasing them around, stuffing what she could get into her coat pockets. Frank did likewise, but it was impossible to get many. By now they were strewn all over the hillside like confetti. From above, they heard the sound of dislodged stones colliding with rocks poking above the soil, followed by men's voices.

"Merde! They're coming. Let's try over there," said Delphine.

The two of them slipped and slid their way into a nearby ravine. Spotting an opening ahead of them, Frank took Delphine's hand and led her into the entrance of a cave. In an unwelcome embrace, dimness and dampness enveloped them

Cold water dripped from the roof, finding its way down their necks no matter how far they bent over in their attempt to avoid it. Several metres in, they hid behind where the wall jutted out and waited. Behind them, the cave continued into utter blackness.

It wasn't long until they heard the gruff, staccato words of their pursuers. The talking stopped, leaving only the sound of footsteps which created a sinister echo bouncing off the cave walls. Then only silence, save for the dripping of water.

Frank tried not to breathe. If they were discovered, that would be it. These people weren't amateurs like him. They'd already tried to kill them once. They wouldn't fail a second time.

Delphine put her hand on his arm in an effort to calm him. Nerves of steel were required at a moment like this. Something she suspected Frank didn't have.

Time seemed to come to a halt. Frank wanted to sit and take the weight off his trembling legs but he daren't move a muscle for fear of alerting them. How long was this going to last? Would death be quick or would they suffer torture? These men must be furious now that the money was as scattered as the wind. Frank wished he'd never left his mundane, predictable existence.

After what seemed an age, the voices resumed, becoming fainter. Their hunters left the cave.

"Thank God," sighed Frank.

"Yes, it didn't go quite as planned."

"That's an understatement. We'd better get going and make our way back to town."

It was long gone nightfall when they arrived exhausted at Delphine's hotel, both looking thoroughly dishevelled.

"You better stay here tonight. You can sleep on the sofa."

Frank accepted. He was homeless now, his beloved Brunhild smashed and broken on a rocky hillside.

They remained in the room all evening. Apart from their cuts, which were superficial, and some bruises that would be visible by morning, they were unhurt.

"I'm never doing that again," said Frank feeling every one of his sixty-five years.

"Next time it'll be easier."

"There won't be a next time."

"Did you always give up, Frank? Give up when things got a little difficult?"

"I wouldn't describe nearly dying as things getting a little difficult."

"We're alive and will live to fight another day."

"You can. My fighting days are over."

"That's not what Churchill would've said."

"Churchill? What has he got to do with it? We bit off more than we could chew. You do whatever you like. But on your own."

Neither said anything for a long while. Delphine was the first to speak.

"What will you do now?"

"Head for home, I suppose."

"That's such a shame. Can you wait a few days?"

"Why?"

"I have an idea and you won't need to do anything. Have you got enough money to stay a few days more?"

"Yes, but I don't feel safe here any longer. They could still be looking for us."

"I understand. Tomorrow I'll put you on the train which goes along the coast. You can go to Ventimiglia in Italy. It's just beyond Menton. No one's going to come looking for you there. I'll meet you there in a week, in front of the cathedral at noon."

"For what?"

"You'll see."

"I don't know, I should be going home."

"What's another few days, and you haven't seen Italy yet. You can take a train along their coast. It's beautiful. You're probably never coming back so you should see it while you can."

Frank wrinkled his nose while he thought about it. "All right, I will. It'll be nice to see a bit of Italy before going home. And sightsee without being shot at."

Ventimiglia was nothing like its French neighbour. The glamour of the Cote d'Azur stopped at the border. The town was like the poor cousin of Menton, scruffier and earthier. But the warmth of the locals made up for the lack of film star looks.

In the cafes and restaurants Frank was greeted enthusiastically, unlike the offhand imperiousness of most French waiters he had encountered, who made you feel as though you were a nuisance rather than a customer.

Buying an English newspaper, Frank took the time to catch up on what had been happening in the world. The communist regimes across Eastern Europe had collapsed like a pack of cards. Even Nicolae Ceausescu, the president of Romania was gone. He and his wife executed by a firing squad after a show trial lasting an hour. In their winter coats, and she in her headscarf, they looked like two hapless pensioners, not the brutal dictators they were.

The Iron Curtain had fallen quicker than anyone could have foreseen. Europe had undergone a greater transformation than anything since the Second World War, and with barely a shot being fired. Unlike Hungary in 1956 or Czechoslovakia in 1968, Russian tanks had been absent from the streets. The expected crackdown on the protesters never came.

Mrs Thatcher, the British Prime Minister, was expressing opposition to talk of German reunification. Frank wondered if she might not be right. After all, Germany had started two world wars in the twentieth century. A divided Germany was a country unable to do that again.

But then if the Wall hadn't come down, he would still be languishing in prison. And today's West Germany was a model of self-restraint, aware of its past and much less gung-ho about going to war than Britain or France.

One day, Frank took the train down to San Remo, Italy's own Monte Carlo, although on a more modest scale.

Out of interest, he bought a road map of Italy. His atlas had been lost with Brunhild. That evening back in his Pensione he examined the map, planning routes he could have taken.

The day Delphine was due to meet him, he got to the cathedral early. It didn't look like one. An ancient stone structure without any spire or tower. Its simplicity inside and out somehow made it impressive. A stone edifice which had stood for nearly a thousand years.

Frank wondered what Delphine had planned. Probably some other barmy scheme to relieve someone of their money and give him a share so he could travel a while longer. Well, she could forget that. He wanted no part of it, he'd had enough. Crime didn't pay.

And without Brunhild, travelling wouldn't be the same. Frank didn't enjoy staying in hotels on his own. It made him feel alone in a way which living in Brunhild didn't. Nor did he particularly like taking trains. He loved the flexibility of the open road, the excitement of finding what was around the next bend, and turning down a side road whenever he wanted.

After a lifetime of no spontaneity, Brunhild had changed his perspective. He grieved her loss as if she were human. Now he knew why Erika had hugged her.

Delphine was late. She seemed excited when she arrived, though as that was her normal state, Frank didn't think anything of it.

"I have a late Christmas present for you," she beamed as she offered her cheeks for kissing.

"That's very kind but I haven't got anything for you."

"I don't want anything. Come," she said grabbing his hand and leading him around the corner.

"Well, I'll be damned…I…I don't know what to say. I'm flabbergasted. You could knock me down with a feather. That's brilliant, just brilliant."

With a red ribbon tied around her and finished in a bow at the front, stood his dear Brunhild.

"How? Where?"

"I got a garage to recover her and take her to a workshop I know in Nice. She wasn't that badly damaged, only a few dents and smashed windows. She needed a new door and a respray. I went for olive green this time. Do you like it?"

"I love it, but it must have cost a fortune. How can I ever repay you?"

"No need. It wasn't too bad. I'm so glad you're pleased. Now you can continue your travels. You'll find a few thousand francs hidden in a pillowcase in the cupboard. I got you all new bedding too. What you had was going mouldy."

"Where on earth did you get the money?"

"Do you really want to know?" Delphine raised her eyebrows in a playful way.

"No, you're right. I don't need to know. But thank you, Delphine. I'm right chuffed."

"Chuffed?"

"It means delighted. And I am. Let me give you a smacker."

"A what?"

"A big, wet sloppy kiss." Frank put his arms out and puckered his lips.

Delphine backed away. "No thanks. You've no idea how many of those I've had to endure in my career."

"Can I buy you some lunch then?"

"Yes, I'd be - how do you say - chuffed."

They chose a small trattoria in the old town. A roaring fire kept the cold of January at bay. It was a cosy refuge, smelling of herbs and meat slowly cooking.

"I didn't know you spoke Italian as well," said Frank after Delphine ordered.

"It's my mother tongue."

"But I thought you were French."

"There's a lot you don't know about me."

Delphine looked straight at him as if her eyes were interrogating his soul, seeking to confirm that she could trust him to keep a secret.

"Are you familiar with the Peter Sarstedt song 'Where do you go to my lovely?'"

"Yes. One of the few pop songs I actually liked. A big hit in the late '60s if I remember correctly. A song about a woman who lives the high life in Paris mixing with the wealthy. Then at the end, you find she grew up in the backstreets of Naples."

"Exactly. I cried when I first heard it."

CHAPTER 18

Violetta looked down on the street below filled with rubble from last night's bombing, wondering if it was too far to jump down onto it and then climb down from there.

"Come away from the edge," called her mother. "You need to be careful now that we have no wall."

Like a doll's house which has been opened so it can be played with, the apartment block had lost its entire frontage. The rest of it still stood. Its inhabitants had survived another Allied air raid by spending the night in the fetid atmosphere of the tunnels which were once the ancient Roman city upon which today's old town stood.

From now on the family's living space would be permanently open to the elements. However, Neapolitans lived in the street, especially during summer evenings when the scorching sun had sunk sufficiently to provide welcome shadow. It was Violetta's favourite time of year. She got to run around with friends until midnight, if not later. That was she had until the Nazis came.

Everyone here lived cheek by jowl, crammed

into poorly maintained old buildings in a maze of narrow streets. Violetta waved at her friend Marina across the narrow gap which separated them. The apartment where she lived still had a small balcony with iron railings, just like Violetta's family also had before last night. A place to hang washing from and shout to neighbours to impart and receive the latest gossip.

The rubble below had brought with it a strange sound. One which Violetta wasn't accustomed to. Silence. With the street blocked by a pile of debris a couple of metres high, motorbikes could no longer get along the alley, buzzing day and night like angry wasps.

"We have no water," tutted Signora Donati when she turned on the tap. "Take the bucket down to the well by the church and get me some."

When Violetta got there, she couldn't see the well for people. A woman told her that other parts of the city were also experiencing problems. There were rumours that the bombing had knocked out the entire water supply of Naples. It took Violetta over an hour to get her turn.

Violetta hated the war. It had taken her father away when she was only ten. She remembered her last hug. He lifted her off the ground and promised he would be back for her birthday. He never made it home. Killed fighting in Greece, they were told.

Naples had become a city of women and old men. Most males who weren't elderly were away fighting or dead.

There were the Nazis of course, but they didn't seem like humans to Violetta. They never smiled or talked to people. They barked their words in German, a language which sounded harsh and ugly to her ears. She would run in the opposite direction whenever she saw one. They frightened her.

That evening, she sat eating a small bowl of spaghetti with her mother and two elder brothers, Gino and Alfredo.

"The Germans have issued a decree today," said Gino. "All men remaining in the city aged eighteen to thirty-three must report to them immediately to be sent to labour camps in the north of Italy or Germany."

"Oh no, I can't bear to lose you too," cried la Signora.

"I'm not going," said Gino.

"Well, we must hide you."

"No, Mama. People are getting ready to rise up. What choice do they have, now that Mussolini's troops have fled and handed the city to the Nazis? Me and Gino are joining them," said Alfredo who, at two years younger than his brother, was only sixteen.

"But that's so dangerous. And you know what they've said. Every German soldier killed will be avenged a hundred times, and the neighbourhood of the fighter will be razed to the ground. Why can't you flee south to Salerno where they say the British and Americans are? Wait it out there until,

God willing, they drive the Germans out."

"No, we are men, not cowards," replied Gino.

"You are still boys, just teenagers."

Gino thrust out his jaw. "Our minds are made up. We will be back before morning."

"But there's a curfew. They'll shoot you on sight."

"They won't see us, we grew up here. Remember how you couldn't find us when you used to come out calling us in for bed when we were younger?"

"Ah, yes," Signora Donati smiled briefly, remembering when life was good, when everything seemed permanent and unchanging. "Such happy days. Make sure you come back, your sister and I need you."

She stood and hugged them tightly, reluctant to let them go not knowing if they would ever return. After a few moments, they extricated themselves from her embrace.

Though sent to bed, Violetta didn't sleep until she heard her mother give thanks to the Madonna in the painting on their wall that her brothers had come home that night.

The next few days were ones of great turmoil as Neapolitans rose up against their oppressors. Fearful for her daughter's safety, her mother forbade her to leave the apartment, and instead went herself to fetch water.

But curiosity got the better of Violetta. She went downstairs and once outside climbed the hill of rubble which blocked the street and sauntered off in the opposite direction from the well. The sporadic gunfire she'd heard from the apartment grew louder.

In a square up ahead Violetta could see a tank, its turret rotating while it sought out targets. But it was a beached shark. It couldn't get down the narrow streets to attack those who were firing. They were quick and nimble, disappearing into the protective maze of alleyways whenever they were threatened.

"Violetta, what are you doing here? Go home."

Gino's face and clothes were covered in grime, his eyes wild with both fear and exhilaration. He no longer looked like the brother whose eyes danced with fun and mischief.

"I wanted to see what was going on."

"Well, now you have. It's not safe, leave before you get hurt."

Violetta scurried away but not home like she should have. She went off down another alley to investigate what else she could see.

The force of a sudden explosion knocked Violetta off her feet and onto her back. Looking up, she watched large pieces of masonry detach themselves from the top of the building directly above her. In the nick of time she got to her knees and crawled under a cafe table next to her.

A deafening noise, louder than the thunderclaps of a summer storm when lightning tore up the sky, jarred her ears. Violetta shook, praying to San Gennaro, the patron saint of Naples, and wishing she had obeyed her mother. After a while it became quiet, but she couldn't see anything for dust. As it gradually settled, her predicament revealed itself. Violetta was entombed. The cafe table had saved her, however she was trapped with no way out.

She shouted for help until her voice was hoarse. No one heard her. Every so often, there was an ominous noise when the debris above her rearranged itself, like tremors after an earthquake. She was too terrified to cry.

How long she was there, she didn't know. It must have been a day, maybe two. At some point she passed out.

When she came to, she sensed space and her world felt soft. A pillow and a bed were beneath her. There was a strange smell too, but not an unpleasant one. Peppermint, perhaps.

She raised her head. Rows of beds were all around her, filled with men. Violetta heard people talking. She couldn't understand them. But they weren't Germans, she was sure of that.

A man in a white coat came over and spoke to her. Realising she had no idea what he was saying, he called over another man in uniform.

"You were found under the rubble," he explained to her in Italian. "But you're not hurt, only severely dehydrated. You'll be able to go home tomorrow. Get some rest for now."

Violetta noticed the tube attached to her arm and the bag on a stand next to the bed feeding her a solution intravenously. Everything became bright and her head spun. She let it fall back onto the pillow.

The next day, they gave her some food and then told her she could leave. One of the soldiers pressed a small package into her hand. 'Gum' he called it. She sniffed it, it smelled of peppermint. By now she knew the Germans had fled and the Americans had arrived.

Crossing the city, she was sad to see the destruction was even worse than before. In addition to the devastation wreaked by the bombing, many buildings not already hit were blackened skeletons, hollowed out from fires.

An old man leaning on his stick and observing the look of horror in her eyes, called out to her.

"Those bastard Germans destroyed as much as they could before they left. They blew it up or burned it down."

It was an apocalyptic scene. Her city, her beautiful city, in ruins.

As she got closer to home, Violetta began to worry what her mother would say. How angry would she be with her? Hopefully, she would be so happy to see her daughter alive she wouldn't be upset with her for long.

Violetta swallowed hard and began to climb the staircase, rehearsing her apology while she did so. A face leaned over the bannister above her.

"Violetta!"

CHAPTER 19

It was Signora Ciccone from the apartment next to her mother's.

"Praise God. We thought you were dead. Come in here a moment, your Mama isn't at home. Come in and sit with me."

She sat Violetta down on a dining chair and knelt down before her, taking her hands in hers. Her grip was tight and her hands clammy. Violetta's heart began beating rapidly. Something was wrong.

"My dear child, I have some terrible news. Your Mama…" The woman choked on a sob. "Your poor Mama is dead."

Dead. The word travelled through Violetta like a spear. Her face crumpled. She pulled her hands away from Signora Ciccone and dropped her face into them and cried.

"What happened?" she asked, looking up red-eyed when she had recovered enough to speak.

"It was the Nazis. We now know that before they went, they left bombs on timers all over the city. Your mother was out looking for you, passing the post office when one went off. They say she didn't suffer. It was instantaneous so that was a blessing."

The spear of words twisted inside Violetta.

"It's all my fault. If I had stayed at home as she told me to, she would still be alive."

"No, you can't think like that. The war killed her, not you."

A sudden panic seized Violetta.

"Where are my brothers? Please tell me they are all right."

"They were last time I saw them. They were leaving to go North to fight. It was before the bomb. No one knows quite where they are, but I'm sure you'll hear from them soon."

"You mean they don't know what happened?"

"No, how could they?"

"I must go."

"Why not stay here a while? I would offer you some food but we have none. Everyone is hungry. They're refusing to let the fishing boats go out. I don't know why. People are walking out into the country to try and find plants they can eat."

"I need some time alone."

"There's something else, my child. The authorities are demanding we all move out tomorrow. They say the building could collapse at any moment."

"But where do we go?"

"That they have no answer for. You should go to your uncle's. He isn't far from here, I'm sure he will take care of you."

Violetta hardly slept that night. This place where

she'd lived all her life would be only a memory tomorrow as already were her mother and father. She wished she too had died. This world was too cruel, its brutality too much to bear.

Violetta's guilt was overwhelming. It crushed her like the rubble beneath which she had been trapped, making her gasp for breath. How could she ever face her brothers after what had happened? Nor could she face her uncle.

For a long while, her tears flowed freely. When they stopped, she'd resolved she must disappear. It would be her punishment for the awful outcome she'd caused.

She joined the many now living on the streets and by their wits. Bed became the hard ground under an archway.

Violetta soon became adept at stealing food from market stalls. Naples had always been a lawless place. Now it was a kleptocracy of the highest order. Statues, icons, even manhole covers were taken. She was merely one of the thousands who were pickpockets and thieves, trying to find a way to survive.

One day in late autumn, she spotted a suave looking gentleman in a green coat made of the finest wool. She noticed him pay for his coffee and carelessly place his wallet in his outside coat pocket when he left the cafe. Now expert pilferer, she followed him, unobserved. Sensing her moment she made her move, slipping her hand inside his pocket. In a second, she had it and turned to run.

"Hey!" The man grabbed a large clump of her unruly, uncombed hair.

"What do you think you're doing?"

"Let me go." She pulled and wriggled but it was no use. His grasp was too strong.

"Where do you live?" he demanded, snatching back his wallet.

"Nowhere."

"What do you mean nowhere?"

"I live on the street."

"Do you like that?"

"Of course not, it's horrible."

He released her hair. She would normally have run but the man displayed compassion in his expression while he surveyed Violetta in her frayed and dirty clothes.

"I need help in my business. A cleaner. Did you want to come and work for me? Food and a room are included. How old are you?"

"Seventeen," lied Violetta, although she could pass for such.

"What do you say? It has to be better than living out here, in danger every day."

Violetta nodded.

He led her to an old villa in one of the better parts of the city. Violetta knew what the establishment was the moment she walked inside but she didn't flinch. What else was she going to do? The alternative was to spend the coming winter outside.

The man addressed a woman reclining on a red couch against a wall of flaking rose pink paint. The woman appeared untouched by the war, wearing makeup and dressed in a fine silk robe of large and colourful flowers.

"Maria, this is - what did you say your name was?"

"Maddalena."

Violetta no longer wished to be known for who she was. That person died the day she learned her mother died because of her.

"Maria, can you sort Maddalena out. Give her some pretty clothes and take her under your wing. I told her she could clean, and that'll be fine if that's all she wants to do.

"Of course, Antonio. Come with me, Maddalena. We'll make you prettier than a Neapolitan beauty queen."

Violetta was relieved finally to be able to wash properly, wiping away the accumulated filth of weeks spent sleeping rough. She relished feeling clean for the first time in months and marvelled at the fine underwear and dress which Maria produced. Maria sat her down in front of a mirror to add the finishing touches.

"Antonio has a very good eye for potential," said Maria standing back to admire her handiwork. "You are a stunning beauty, my dear."

Violetta hardly recognised the face which stared back at her. Her hair combed and styled in the fashion of the day, her lips the reddest of red, and her eyelashes now so prominent with mascara.

The street urchin had been replaced by a young woman, a Neapolitan princess.

"Well, you better not wear these for cleaning. Take them off while I find you something more suitable."

Violetta experienced regret. She had never worn pretty things before other than her white dress for her first communion.

"No, I don't want to clean. I'll do it."

"Do what?"

"What you do."

"Are you sure?"

"Yes, I'm sure."

"Why don't you take a few days to settle in? Think about it, there's no pressure with Antonio."

"No, tomorrow. I'd like to start then."

The first time Violetta was nervous. So was her customer, a young soldier. It got easier after that.

In March 1944, Vesuvius awoke after some seventy years of sleep. It stands only five miles from Naples, dwarfing all around it. A constant reminder that ultimate power remains, like it always has and always will, with nature.

For days there had been rumbles. At night, molten lava could be seen, jettisoned into the night sky like the most spectacular red and orange firework display that could be imagined. Neapolitans flocked to their churches to pray that this wouldn't be the big one.

Then one day a massive explosion brought everyone out onto the streets. It was as if the war was starting all over again. Vesuvius had blown its top and a massive thick purple-black cloud billowed upwards into the sky. Soon ash rained down upon Naples like dirty snow, but snow which wouldn't melt in the sun.

After all the privations heaped upon its citizens in recent years, for some, including Violetta, this was the last straw. Her once vibrant city had turned into a place she barely recognised. A place where just when you thought things couldn't possibly get any worse, they did. Always plagued by malaria, typhoid broke out. It seemed that the misfortunes of the inhabitants would never end.

In June, Rome was liberated. Violetta packed her few belongings and headed to the capital. A life serving up pleasure to men of little means offered no future. She would find those to whom money was no object and live life on her terms, not those of others. Her life seemed destined to be a solitary one so she would make sure that it was at least comfortable.

CHAPTER 20

"Eventually, I found my way to Paris and made my home there and became Delphine."

"Did you ever see your brothers again?" asked Frank.

"No." Delphine slid her index fingers across her eyelids, wiping away tears which would otherwise escape.

"Do you know where they are?"

"I heard from a friend that they returned to Napoli. They believe I'm dead, it's better that way."

"Do you truly believe that?"

"Yes. Look, everyone's gone. We're the last ones here. We should go so the owners can have a break before the dinner crowd arrive."

They walked to Brunhild.

"Can I give you a lift anywhere?"

"Yes, to the station. I'm returning to France. Where will you go?"

"I thought I might drive down the coast, all the way to Sicily."

"You'll enjoy that. There are many beautiful things to see in my country."

Frank didn't want them to part.

"You could come with me."

"Me in a camper van? No, I'm not suited for such a life."

Noticing how disappointed Frank appeared, Delphine made a suggestion.

"How about if we meet in Capri the first weekend of March? I know a wonderful place to stay there."

"That would be lovely."

"Meet me in the town square by the clock at one in the afternoon on the first Saturday of the month."

They reached the station. Delphine went to get out but hesitated.

"Do you think less of me, now that you know my story?"

"No, quite the opposite."

"Thank you for being so non-judgmental. Arrivederci, Frank."

He watched her go. A lonely person, like him.

Frank was spellbound by Italy. He had never been anywhere with so many historic buildings. Even the smallest town was replete with them.

He also fell in love with la dolce vita. Now willing to stray beyond his previous knowledge of Italian food, pizza and spaghetti Bolognese, he found endless pleasure in dining out. French food had been a little fussy for his tastes. In Italy, they were able to conjure the most flavoursome of meals out of the simplest of ingredients.

"It's because we buy locally," explained a waiter. "The food is always fresh."

Frank thought back to his frozen TV dinners for one back home that looked appealing on the packaging but tasted so bland. Italian cuisine reminded him of when he was younger, before supermarkets homogenised everything into cheap and tasteless. A time when tomatoes possessed real flavour, and eggs were the brightest of yellow. Those things were still the case here in Italy.

Taking his time, he made his way down the coast, diverting inland to see Florence and meander around Tuscany before moving onto Rome and then Naples to catch a boat to Capri. Not feeling brave enough to face the traffic of Naples, Frank left Brunhild in a town close by and caught a train into the city.

It wasn't immediately attractive like the other Italian cities he'd seen. However, looking beyond the veneer of dirt and decay, he found much charm and character. Naples wasn't a refined lady like Florence or a classic beauty like Rome, more an unruly old relative who had lived a life of debauchery and had no intention of letting age mellow her.

Frank spent a few days walking the streets and getting to know Naples. It was the most lively city he'd been to, turbocharged by the Neapolitans themselves who displayed passion in everything they did.

With the noise, the chaos, and the crowded streets, Naples demanded to be noticed. When the frenetic atmosphere became too much, Frank would retreat to the waterfront and sit with his legs dangling over the edge, soaking in the incomparable Bay of Naples, crowned by the dramatic outline of Vesuvius.

Naples was bursting with architectural and archaeological treasures, although little attempt was made to showcase them as in the tourist honeypots further north. Nothing here had the iconic status of Rome's colosseum or Pisa's leaning tower. It made the unexpected gems, of which there were several, even more satisfying to discover. One of the world's oldest cities, the Greeks founded it as Neapolis, or new city, nearly two and a half thousand years earlier. Today's Naples is built over a honeycomb of the old Greek and Roman towns and the catacombs.

Frank had gone native while he travelled down Italy. No longer a fan of milky tea with two sugars, he preferred the bitter taste and delicious aroma of an espresso, and a glass of lively Italian red to a beer. In Naples, he added a local snack to his list of favourite foods, the sfogliatella, a clam shaped pastry filled with sweetened ricotta and eaten at breakfast time.

On the day of his departure, a morning fog brought a sharp chill to the air when Frank boarded the ferry. There was an eerie stillness to the ocean and mist enveloped the boat. Fog horns vied for attention from boats which were close by but invisible. Frank wondered if the captain had radar, or if he was navigating by the seat of his pants and hoping for the best. From what he'd seen so far of the Italian attitude to risk, Frank decided it was probably the latter.

Capri emerged like a lost world out of the fog when the sun burned it off. Sheer rock faces of white thrust skywards above the green vegetation below, amongst which were scattered houses painted white.

Not appreciating it was a five hundred foot climb up to the town, Frank ignored the calls of taxi drivers and followed the signpost and steps. He stopped frequently to get his breath back. The view across the sea to Naples and Vesuvius was spectacular and made the climb worthwhile.

It was gone one o'clock when he reached the small square. Delphine was already waiting beneath the clock tower.

"You look exhausted. Tell me you didn't walk up," she laughed.

"I was almost on all fours by the end of it."

"I'm not surprised. Only the English would be mad enough to do that. Let's go find some lunch so you can recover."

"Well, this is a very expensive looking town," said Frank as they sat down, having already noted the many top fashion brand shops lining the streets.

"Yes, it's a big hit with film stars and the like, and such a pretty island. I have been here many times. I've got us a small villa for the weekend. I thought we could wander around and enjoy the ambience."

"That sounds great but you must let me pay half."

"Even if you sold Brunhild, which I wouldn't want you to, it wouldn't be enough. Please don't feel bad. Like I've said before, money is always something I can get more of. The company of someone I like being with not necessarily so."

Frank's heart beat a little faster. He wondered if he was falling in love with her. Could it be that she felt the same?

After lunch, Delphine led him along a narrow alley and into what looked like an ordinary house from the front.

"Come this way, I think you might like it."

Delphine led him along a dark corridor and opened the door at the far end.

"Wow!" exclaimed Frank.

The room was spacious, modern and minimalist, and furnished in white. However, Frank's comment wasn't about the room but the view through the patio windows. Beyond the outside deck, the ground ended with a low wall before disappearing into the Mediterranean far below. As far as the eye could see was a cobalt sea until it collided with the vertiginous Amalfi coast.

"Why don't you sit down outside while I make us some coffee?"

Frank sat drinking in the vista. He had seen some impressive sights these past few months, but this had to be the best one.

"Do you mind if I ask you something?" said Frank when she returned.

"I don't know. Should I mind?"

"Maybe it's not my place to say so but we're less than an hour's boat ride from Naples. Indeed, you must have done it yourself."

"No, I've never been back there. An old acquaintance had me flown here direct from the airport by helicopter."

"What I'm trying to say is…"

"Yes?"

"I was thinking why don't you go back and see your brothers? I'm sure they'd be overjoyed to see you. I've been wondering how I could repay you for repairing Brunhild so when I was in Naples, I did some research and made some enquiries. I found out where they live."

"Really. And what business of it was yours?" Delphine challenged him, her cheeks flaring pink . "I didn't reveal my most intimate secrets so that you could become my therapist. What do you know about how they feel or how I feel?"

"I thought you'd be pleased."

"Well, you were wrong. Enjoy the view. I'm going to take a nap."

CHAPTER 21

Frank was left sitting alone, confused why his attempt to make her happy produced the reaction it had. Resting his head against the back of the sun lounger he fell asleep.

The opening of the patio doors woke him. Delphine stood before him. Her manner had softened.

"I'm sorry, Frank, for turning on you like that." She sat down next to him. "You didn't deserve it. But I can't see them. Not after what I did, after what I became. Can't you see that?"

"Not really. If I were them, I would want to see you. I'd be so glad to know you were alive."

"Perhaps you're right about them, but the shame is too much for me. What can I tell them I've done with my life? What will their children think of their aunt? At the moment, they must all idolise my memory, my brothers recounting tales of the sweet little sister who perished and who is now in heaven."

"You could pretend I was your husband," volunteered Frank.

"What?"

Frank shrunk into his chair, embarrassed by the absurdity of his suggestion.

"You would do that for me?"

He couldn't go back on his offer now. "Yes, if it means that you can see your family again."

"You're such a good man, Frank. Maybe that is the answer. We could go and visit them together."

"Er…I…"

"Don't worry. It will be easy for you. I'm sure they still can't speak English. You won't have to say anything. I can do all the talking. Just like she always does, you're probably thinking," joked Delhine.

"No, not at all," said Frank, already regretting his rash offer.

Delphine was animated, almost skittish, like a teenager.

"I should call them now, before I have time to change my mind. Do you have their address?"

"Yes."

"Good. I'll be able to find them in the telephone directory."

"Here it is." Frank handed her a piece of paper taken from his pocket.

Frank could tell she'd been crying when she came out again but joy was written large across her face.

"I spoke to them both. We were all crying down the phone. I explained how I was so ashamed Mama died because she'd gone out looking for me. They said they didn't blame me one bit, and to hear from

me again is a gift from God. It was so wonderful."
The emotion of it all became too much for her. Frank stood up and put his arms around her. After a few moments, Delphine recovered her composure.

"They've asked us for lunch tomorrow. Their wives and their children and their partners will be there. I'm so thrilled but so nervous at the same time. It's been over forty years. Thank you for making me do this, Frank. You're my hero."

Frank swelled with pride. Everything was turning out well. She would be reunited with her long-lost family and ever grateful to him, a gratitude which could turn to love.

"What did you say about me?"

"That you were a businessman and had to come to Rome for a conference, and we were spending the weekend in Capri beforehand. And that you had finally persuaded me to contact them."

"We should probably get the story of 'us' straight before we meet them."

"Of course. It will be no problem, deception has been my life's career."

The following morning, Delphine played with the ring she had put on her wedding finger for the entire duration of the boat journey. Frank was anxious too. He tried to imagine how much more apprehensive she must feel on this momentous occasion, but it did little to calm his nerves. Stop being such a wimp, he scolded himself. All he had to do was sit there and smile inanely. For once, he was pleased he only spoke English.

They took a taxi from the port. Delphine didn't talk. She faced the window, breathing in the city which she once knew so well and whose very essence ran through her veins.

She asked the driver to stop at the end of the street. "I can't believe I am actually here, and that Gino is living only a street away from where we lived when we were children. His street escaped the bombing. It's as if I'm walking back into my past."

"Do you need a moment?"

"No, it's all right. Come on."

She held his hand to steady herself in her high heels while they walked along the cobbles. Playing children ran around them. Old ladies looked down from their balconies, like hawks surveying the comings and goings in the neighbourhood. Some shouted across the narrow alleyway to exchange news with a neighbour on their balcony on the opposite side. Vespas weaved around the pedestrians with frightening speed but somehow managed to avoid running anyone over.

Ahead of them, Frank noticed two men dressed in their Sunday best, their black hair, now streaked with grey, greased back. He looked at Delphine who nodded.

She let go of his hand and hurried towards their open arms. The siblings hugged and kissed repeatedly in between their crying. Spontaneous applause broke out from those on their balconies and in the street. Frank wiped his eyes. Even he couldn't hold back tears watching the family reunion.

Next, it was his turn. The two brothers approached him, their arms outstretched, taking it in turns to embrace him and kiss him on both cheeks. They said something in Italian and one beckoning with his hand, led them up the concrete staircase to the second floor.

The door into the apartment was flung open by one of the brothers and they were hit by a wall of sound. It was that loud and joyful noise Italians make when they are in groups, all talking at once. Gesticulating and jostling for position, they pushed past each other and surged forward to greet the couple.

The room, not spacious to begin with, was mostly filled by a large table covered in antipasti. Frank lost count of how many kissed him. Even though each said their name slowly and deliberately for his benefit as though he were hard of hearing, he failed to retain any idea of who was who apart from Delphine's two brothers.

There wasn't enough room for all of them to stand and talk. Alfredo shouted above the noise to get everybody to sit. Delphine was squeezed in between her two brothers at the head of the table and Frank physically steered to a place on the side.

There was a great deal of shouting when one of the women went to sit in the empty chair to his left. Reprimanded, she moved down to the far end of the table. Frank was left pondering why no one had been allowed to sit there. His question was answered when a late arrival, a young man, sat down next to him and shook his hand.

"Hello, I'm Eduardo. Gino's grandson. I sit here because I speak some English."

The sound of a fork on a wine glass interrupted him. Alfredo was standing again and talking. Eduardo translated for Frank.

"He says today is the happiest day of his life. God has finally granted his wish to see his sister again. He makes a toast to Violetta and you."

In the confined space it was impossible for everyone, once seated, to stand up again so the guests remained in their chairs, clinking glasses with those nearest to them as they all beamed and repeated "Violetta e Franco." Then without further ado, everyone dived into the food and noise level maximum resumed while they talked, mostly all at the same time.

Frank looked down the table at Delphine. He had never seen her this happy. It was indeed a joyous occasion. These people may not be materially wealthy but Frank could see that they were rich. Rich in happiness and their love for each other.

The food and wine kept on coming. Eduardo talked mainly to the young woman on the other side of him, which suited Frank who was pleased to keep a low profile. He drank more than he should.

Eduardo tapped him lightly on his arm to get his attention and pointed towards Alfredo who was leaning forwards in his direction.

"He asks where you met."
"Delphine and me? We-"
"Delphine?"
He heard Alfredo repeat the name loudly.

CHAPTER 22

Delphine who was chatting to Gino stopped talking. Her face became pale as if she had seen a ghost. Alfredo turned towards her and began talking in an excitable manner, but this time not in a cheerful way. She stumbled over her words of reply, more so as he became louder and seemingly angrier about whatever she was telling him.

The rest of the table fell silent. Everybody was looking at her, their mouths agape. She pushed her chair back, said something fast and furious to her brother, and hurried past those seated and out of the door.

With her gone, all eyes turned on Frank. The warmth and bonhomie had evaporated. He didn't need to be asked.

"I better go too," he said wiggling his chair backwards so that he could get up.

Out on the street, Delphine was half running, half walking.

"I'm so sorry," he said catching up with her.

"I need to leave this place. I should never have come here. I don't know what on earth I was thinking." She threw her arms up in the air in anger and frustration.

It was a sombre journey back to Capri. Delphine said nothing and Frank didn't know what to say. The island of green and white set in the aquamarine sea and shining in the sun seemed incongruous, completely unsuited to their situation.

Back at the villa, Delphine shut herself in her room. Frank cursed that he hadn't kept his mouth shut. What a stupid idea it had been to say he could go as her husband. Now he'd made things worse, not better.

Delphine, Violetta, Maddalena, whoever she was, reconciled herself to her fate years ago. She had closed that wound. He'd persuaded her to re-open it. She looked so content and fulfilled, briefly back in the warmth of her family. Now that had all unravelled, making things much harder for her than they were before.

Frank sat out on the patio staring into the distance. Why had he really done it? For her or for him? To make her like him? He was an old fool. She was so different to him. Expecting her to fall in love with him if he did her a favour was a fantasy. Time to move on, get to Sicily and then drive home.

When Delphine reappeared the sun was setting and casting a golden glow on the mountains of the mainland.

"Look, I-" said Frank standing up.

"There's no need to say anything. It's not your fault. I'll be all right. Life has given me many knocks, but it's the same for everyone. You just have to get back up and get on with it. My taxi will be here shortly to take me to the helicopter. You can stay here tonight if you want. It's paid for until tomorrow."

"I'll probably leave straight after you and drive on to Sicily."

"I'm going to be in Taormina on the east coast of Sicily in two weekend's time. Did you want to have lunch maybe? One last time, for old time's sake. I could meet you in Piazza IX Aprile by the horological tower. Ask at the tourist office if you have trouble finding it."

"Yes, if you're sure you still want to talk to me."

"Don't be silly, of course I do. I'll be there at one o'clock."

The doorbell rang.

"My taxi. A bientôt."

She offered her cheek to Frank, picked up her suitcase, and left quickly without looking back to wave like she usually did.

It was but a short ferry ride from the toe of Italy to Sicily, but Frank soon realised it was a place apart. Here, Europe and Arabia have both exerted a strong influence. Palermo, the island's capital, was even more anarchic than Naples. Sometimes described as a Middle Eastern city in Europe and a Norman city in the Mediterranean, it contained some impressive historical sites but in many parts the Mafia had ruined it.

Badly bombed in World War Two, the damage done was left untouched for a long time. Developers controlled by the Mob bribed corrupt officials and tore down many fine buildings, and even paved over parks in the middle of the night. In their place, they threw up apartment blocks of questionable construction. Ugly in places, the city nonetheless enjoyed a splendid location by a bay of turquoise and dark blue water and beneath Monte Pellegrino.

From Palermo, Frank and Brunhild continued westwards on their anticlockwise circumnavigation of the island, planning to end up in Taormina back near to where the boat from the mainland had arrived. Medieval villages and Greek and Roman ruins were commonplace. A warm wind blowing from the South seemed to whisper of Africa, whose coastline was less than a hundred miles distant.

Although it was only March, the weather was as good as an English summer's day and with more sunshine to boot. Wildflowers of red, orange, purple, and yellow carpeted much of the countryside. Once again, Frank wondered what there was to go home for. The climate rejuvenated him, the aches and pains of damp winters and dark evenings forgotten. Passing smallholdings surrounded by citrus groves, Frank imagined himself buying a modest dwelling. Somewhere with a little land for cultivating produce and on the edge of a town so he could walk in for a drink or to have a meal.

The heat would doubtless be intense come summer, but he could live in the shade. He could see that the old houses with their thick stone walls and shutters were built to remain cool in summer. And better the sun than the weather of home. Waking up to blue skies most days this past winter had made Frank a happier person. The often relentless grey cloud of the England had sapped him of energy, and made him feel permanently lethargic.

The language would be a problem but he could learn. It would be something to keep his brain active. At home he had been vegetating, letting his horizons narrow even more than they already had. His world had been shrinking all the time. Travel gave him a confidence he previously lacked and broadened his mind, made him receptive to new experiences and to seeing a challenge as an opportunity rather than something to be avoided.

Over the course of the next few days, Frank came to the conclusion that he should spend some time living here first. Then, if it proved to be a success, he could sell his place in England and use the proceeds to acquire a property on the island. Of course, there'd be plenty of people telling him he'd lost his marbles. But those were the same people who poured cold water on his trip in the first place, and now he knew they were wrong.

Perhaps Delphine would come and visit him and

maybe also fall under the island's spell. How long could she keep doing what she did? She wasn't much younger than him. She couldn't live on her looks or live life in the fast lane forever.

Frank's daydreaming came crashing back to earth when he remembered he was almost out of money. Money, or lack of it, always got in the way of plans. He wouldn't have needed much for a few months extra here, but he didn't have it.

Unless... one last venture with Delphine would be all it would take to get a spare thousand or two. They could be less ambitious this time, something easy. It was either that or give up on his dream and go home. He had been right to take his trip, and he would be right to try living here.

Taormina was perched high above the sea. It was sparkling seductively in the sunlight the day Frank arrived. Inland, and still covered with snow on its upper reaches, the sprawling mass of Mount Etna, Europe's most active volcano, belched smoke into the air. It had made a dramatic backdrop to Frank's journey for some time now, dominating the eastern side of Sicily.

The town of Taormina, while undeniably beautiful, was a little too sanitised for Frank's taste. Touring Sicily, he'd grown to love the less manicured towns which were typical of the island. He could see immediately why Delphine would enjoy Taormina with its fancy boutiques and luxury hotels.

Changing into clothes that she would approve of,

he made his way to the square and the clock tower. Reliable as ever she soon appeared. Her reality was even better than his memory of her. She exuded an aura he couldn't quite describe or define but it gave him butterflies in his stomach like a schoolboy falling in love for the first time.

They ate lunch outside, watching the world go by. Delphine quizzed him about his travels. Neither mentioned Naples. Intuitively, Frank sensed that subject would always be off limits.

The conversation was one-sided. Although he'd already known Delphine for over four months and knew things about her others didn't, leading questions such as "Who are you here with?" or "Have you had any successful steals recently?" didn't seem appropriate.

Frank noticed that Delphine seemed to have lost her sparkle. The melancholy which had always lurked below the surface was more obvious now. He blamed himself for that, for the débacle in Naples.

"How exciting," said Delphine when Frank explained his plan.

"Yes, I've fallen in love with this island. There's only one problem, I'm almost out of money."

"I would gladly give you some, but I've been going through a rather fallow period recently and also spending too much."

"Oh no, I didn't mean that. I would never expect you to. You've always been more than generous. I was wondering, however, whether you... whether we...might do a little wealth redistribution together one last time."

"Of course," Delphine smiled. "It's so much easier when there's two. One to entice and one to implement. This town attracts the wealthy. I'm here with one of them. Bernardo is his name. We have a three room suite at the Grand Hotel Timeo. It's only a few minutes from here, near the Greek theatre. He wanted a companion and he's loaned me a diamond necklace to wear in the evenings. If we take that, I'm sure you'll have more than enough. It's got to be worth two hundred thousand dollars on the black market."

"Two hundred thousand! I don't need that much. Doesn't he have something he would miss a little less?"

"You've got to go big, Frank, or you'll never achieve anything. Anyway, I need my half share. I want to give up this life. I'm tired of having to pretend I enjoy someone's company when I don't. It won't be difficult. Tomorrow when we come down to breakfast, I'll leave the necklace on the coffee table by the sofa. The door will be unlocked. Wait in reception and when you see us enter the dining room, all you need to do is to go up and take it. It's room 500 on the top floor. Just let the door lock behind you when you leave."

"Then what?"

"We won't get the best price if we sell it in Sicily. Can you get to Rome, and meet me there on Wednesday? Eleven o'clock in Piazza Navona by the fountain. I know where to go there to get a good deal."

"All right. You know, with that money, what I get for selling my house, and whatever you may have, we could have a very nice life here in Sicily."

"Frank?" Delphine's brow creased in confusion.

Frank blushed. He'd never thought he would let it spill out like that. Still, he was pleased he had. What point was there at this stage in life in keeping his feelings bottled up like a lovelorn adolescent? And Delphine had said she wanted to abandon her present life. A move to Sicily would let her do exactly that.

"I really like you, Delphine, and I think you're lonely like me. We both deserve a new start."

Delphine sat back in her chair, twirling some of her hair in her fingers while she considered her reply. Frank's heart turned over repeatedly. He feared it must be as loud as Brunhild's engine.

"I like you too, Frank, very much. But as a friend. And a quiet life amongst the olive groves, or picking lemons, it's just not me. I would never want to leave Paris, not again like when I married and went to live in the middle of nowhere. It was too dead for me. I need the big city. I always have and always will."

Although Frank tried to conceal his disappointment, he couldn't hide it. Delphine reached across the table and put her hand on his.

"I'll come and visit you. I promise. Often. I'll visit you often. That is until you meet some wonderful

Sicilian lady and forget about me. Look at the time, I should be going. See you in Rome."

Frank remained seated, his balloon burst. But it hadn't come as a surprise. He hadn't truly expected it to be any different. You could steal a person's jewellery, but you couldn't steal someone's heart, not unless they wanted it stolen.

CHAPTER 23

That evening, Frank walked up to the Greek theatre, hoping a stroll would help relax him. On the way, he passed Delphine's hotel. His stomach tightened when he thought of what he was supposed to do there tomorrow morning.

At over two thousand years old and with an unparalleled setting looking down the eastern coast and towards the cone of Mount Etna, the ruins of the theatre were a special place. But Frank was too wound up to enjoy his visit.

After leaving, he wandered into the Timeo for a look around. Oozing old world charm, it displayed sumptuousness from an age gone by. At the rear, carefully tended gardens interspersed with palm trees gave a breathtaking view of the Ionian Sea. However, Frank remained too distracted to appreciate his surroundings.

The following morning, he was in the lobby early. Taking cover behind a newspaper, he watched the well-heeled guests amble past en route to the terrace for breakfast.

Bernardo arrived with Delphine. He wore a brown

suit and dark glasses. Their design indicated they might be for medical reasons rather than ordinary sunglasses. Delphine hadn't mentioned he would be in a wheelchair. Guilt pricked Frank's conscience at the thought of stealing from an invalid until he reminded himself of Delphine's explanation of how these people acquired their wealth. Why should a wheelchair make a difference? Being confined to one didn't necessarily mean that someone was a good person.

Frank went in search of their room. Delphine had left the door on the latch. It opened onto the sitting area. He went across to the sofa. Exactly as Delphine had said there was a coffee table but no sign of the necklace.

Frank scanned the surfaces. He walked around the room a few times. Nothing. Maybe she'd left it in the bedroom.

He went through the door to his right. Not seeing the necklace anywhere, he began to go through drawers but they were empty. Opening a cupboard, he saw a man's clothes hanging there.

Frank searched the other bedroom. Still nothing. Maybe it was in the safe. Perhaps Delphine had programmed it for the man. He knew which numbers she used. He found the safe in a cupboard in the lounge. With increasingly sweaty hands, Frank tried her code. It didn't work.

He searched the rooms once more but without success. The necklace wasn't here unless it was in the safe.

Frank suddenly realised he'd lost all track of time. It wouldn't be long until they got back. It was time to leave. He opened the door to the corridor.

"Is this what you were looking for?"

A man, who was almost as broad as he was tall, blocked the exit. From his hand, like a snake uncurled and ready to bite, he dangled the diamond necklace.

He dropped it in a pocket of his black suit, producing a pistol from the other pocket.

"Sit down," he demanded.

Frank's legs turned to mush. He walked slowly backwards to the sofa. The man pointed his gun directly at him. His eyes were cold and piercing, someone who appeared to be unlikely to have any compunction about pulling the trigger.

"Now we wait."

Impassive, the man stood opposite him.

Frank's legs began to twitch involuntarily. He pushed his feet firmly on the floor to try and stop the movement and rested his trembling hands on the sofa.

When the door opened, Frank wished he'd shouted at Delphine to run, but by the time the thought occurred to him it was already too late. The minder commanded her to sit on the sofa next to Frank.

"So is this what you do, Delphine?" asked Bernardo in English, moving his wheelchair until he was positioned opposite them and next to his fixer. "Betray people who place their trust in you? Paolo here saw you at the cafe yesterday talking to this man. He overheard what you were planning."

"It's all been an unfortunate mistake," said Frank.

"Indeed it has. However, I wouldn't categorise it as trivial as a mistake."

"Are you going to call the police?" asked Delphine.

"That won't be necessary."

"That's very good of you, sir," said Frank. "We're very grateful, it won't happen again."

Giving him a frown of contempt, Bernardo continued.

"You're right, it won't happen again. I'm going to make sure of that. Paolo, call Gianluca. I want you to take them out on my yacht and make fish food of them."

Frank wanted to get down on his knees and beg for mercy but he restrained himself. Delphine hadn't flinched, she hadn't displayed a single trace of emotion.

What happened next occurred so quickly, Frank wasn't quite sure how it did. She must have taken it from her bag. When Paolo took his focus off them for a couple of seconds to go over to the phone, Delphine shot him in the back of the head.

The man turned. He stood there for a brief moment with a look of utter disbelief that this could be happening before falling face forwards to the floor with a thud, landing at their feet. Frank yelled out in horror.

"And as for you," said Delphine standing up and going over to Bernardo. "You're a crook. Someone who doesn't give a shit about how many people you have killed or why. I've had to spend a lifetime making arseholes like you feel good. But you're not good, you're kind are pure evil."

Frank had never witnessed her so enraged, so full of hatred. Years of suffering and indignity, which Delphine carefully masked beneath the face she showed to the world, had erupted, the pressure of it all finally too much to contain.

She shot Bernardo in the chest several times. His body jerked in a spasm with each bullet as though he was being electrocuted. Then his head slumped down onto his chest and remained there.

Frank jumped up from the sofa.

"Oh my God! Why did you have to kill him too?"

CHAPTER 24

"Because he deserved to die. He was going to have us killed."

"This isn't good," said Frank pushing his hand through what little remained of his hair. "What have we done? What are we going to do?"

Delphine's face was implacable, displaying a ruthless resolve.

"You need to pull yourself together, Frank, and we need to get out of here."

Frozen with shock, he didn't move. Delphine took his hand and led him out into the corridor. Two members of staff came running towards them.

"Stay back," she ordered, brandishing her gun. She pulled Frank in the direction of the emergency exit. "Do you have your keys on you?"

"Yes," replied Frank breathlessly, trying to keep up with her while she hurried down the stairs.

"Let's head to the van then."

Pushing the bar on the emergency exit door at the bottom, they set off a piercing alarm when they emerged from the hotel which caused pigeons picking on discarded food to fly at them and only narrowly miss them.

"Where are you parked?"

"Just outside the town. This way."

Hearing shouting behind them, they turned to look. One of the men from the corridor was pointing at them and a security guard was demanding they stop.

Diverting down a side street, Frank and Delphine imitated a running motion, but it was really no more than a fast walk. They were already exhausted, neither used to physical exercise.

"We're not going to get to the van without being caught," said Delphine. "Let's jump on that bus up ahead in the square."

Delphine discarded the gun, dropping it into a waste bin at the end of the alleyway.

Finding seats a few rows from the back of the bus, Frank willed it to move off before they were found and arrested. After what seemed an age to Frank, its closing door gave a welcome whooshing sound. The bus moved out of Taormina but to where they didn't know. Not until the guide sitting next to the driver spoke, first in Italian and then in English.

"Welcome ladies and gentleman on our tour today to Mount Etna. At over three thousand metres, it is two and a half times the size of Vesuvius, and covers an area of nearly twelve hundred square kilometres. It is Europe's largest and most active volcano…"

"We've done it," whispered Delphine. "We can spend the day up there. We'll have them drop us off outside town near Brunhild when we return tonight and make our getaway."

"Then what?"

"Take the ferry back to the mainland and drive North and out of Italy."

"In case you've forgotten, we're wanted for murder. The Italian police aren't going to give up just because we go back to our homes. One day, there'll be a knock on the door and a copper with an arrest warrant."

"We won't go home. They'll never find us in South America."

"South America? Are you joking?"

"I have contacts in Buenos Aires. They'll help us get established. It's the most European city on the whole continent, often likened to Paris. You'd like it, I'm sure."

"I'd have liked Sicily," said Frank. "A fugitive in South America isn't what I had in mind. I'd never see my family again."

"It's your choice, Frank. You don't have to come."

"Frank?"

Apprehensively, he turned towards the unexpected sound of someone saying his name to see a woman standing by his seat.

"I knew it was you. Helmut, it is him."

Two rows back on the opposite side, Helmut grinned and waved energetically.

"What a small world it is. Hello, I'm Johanna," she said to Delphine.

"Claudette," said Delphine abruptly.

"Madam, could you please sit down," the tour guide called down the bus.

"This is a wonderful coincidence. We must talk later. See you when we get there," said Johanna.

Frank merely nodded, he was too preoccupied to respond.

"Relax, Frank, it'll be too cold to take our clothes off up there," laughed Johanna.

"Who are they?" mouthed Delphine, lines of irritation breaking across her forehead.

"A couple I met in Germany last year."

"Exactly what we don't need right now. Why's she talking about taking your clothes off?"

"I met them in a nudist camp in Germany."

"Well, you do surprise me. You must tell me the whole story sometime."

While the bus followed a twisting road ever higher, the guide explained there would be gondolas to take them up farther, and then trucks to get them to the summit of Etna.

Frank didn't pay any attention to the spectacular views. In his mind, he was constantly replaying the events of this morning. Frank still couldn't believe what had happened. He had never imagined Delphine would kill someone, let alone carry a gun. Something inside her must have snapped, the weight of her past finally too much to bear. Or was it revenge, revenge for all that life had hurled at her?

Either way, it made no difference. Murder was murder whichever way you looked at it. It didn't matter if the man was rich or poor, or even a criminal. Once she had shot Paolo, they'd no longer been in immediate danger. Bernado, trapped in a wheelchair, posed no threat. They had time to make their escape before he could have called for backup.

"We must take the same gondola," called Johanna when they arrived at their destination while she and Helmut followed the other passengers filing off the bus.

"No, you go ahead," said Delphine. "We'll see you up there, I need to attend to something."

"Okay, we'll meet you up top. We're so thrilled to have bumped into you."

"I don't need them bombarding us with questions," said Delphine watching them go.

She and Frank were the last to get off and chose a gondola that was empty. The ascent took them over a black and barren landscape where previous molten lava flows had solidified. The terrain was interspersed with snow.

"It's like being on the moon," said Delphine.

"Or a massive slag heap."

"What's a slag heap?"

"What we have next to our pits at home. The coal mines are all shut down now, but the black hills of mud and rock left over once they took out the coal are still there."

Ahead of them, smoke billowed from craters. It was as if they were the doors to the underworld.

Inside the gondola, it was freezing. They'd left

Taormina without coats, never imagining they would be up at this elevation.

Frank noticed Delphine shiver, but what concerned him more was what had caught his eye below. They both saw them. The lights flashing on the roofs of cars skidding to a halt, and the men running towards the cable car station. Frank's mouth had become as dry as desert sand.

"They've found us," he croaked.

Delphine didn't reply.

Their journey in the gondola was ending. Beneath and ahead of them all was now the blinding white of snow, an effect amplified by the harsh sunlight. Trucks were waiting for the sightseers to transport them to the highest permitted point. A few intrepid hikers were walking it.

There was a jolt. Suddenly, they were out of the sunshine and into shadow when the gondola entered the top station. Slowing right down, its doors slid open.

Delphine looked at Frank as they got out. Her expression was resolute.

"I'm not letting them take me. I'm not going to spend my life in prison."

"We've nowhere to run, Delphine. There's no escape."

"You'll be okay, Frank. Just tell them the truth. You didn't kill anyone. It was me. Tell them about the gun in the waste bin by the square. It's got my fingerprints on it, not yours."

Johanna and Helmut who were waiting for them

stood open-mouthed, unable to believe what they were hearing. Delphine ignored them. She hurried out of the building, crossing the parking area and into the snow. She began wading through it. Soon it was almost up to her knees. That didn't deter her. She was climbing a slope that went in the opposite direction to the track to the summit.

"Frank, what's happening?" called Helmut but Frank didn't reply. He began to ascend after her.

"Delphine! Delphine!" He shouted through the thin air.

She kept on going and disregarded the warning sign. A skull and crossbones.

In his haste to catch up with her, Frank tripped, landing face down. Brushing the snow off his face with his hands, he got back up. Delphine was now a considerable way ahead. Behind him, the police had got off a gondola and were in hot pursuit.

On she went. He followed, still calling Delphine's name. Either she couldn't hear in the strong wind that blew at this altitude or she was pretending not to. She didn't once look back. She was going ever higher up the steep gradient.

After several minutes, Delphine got to where the snow had melted from steam coming out from a side crater. She crossed the uneven rocks, stumbling as she went but still focused on her goal.

Reaching the edge of the crater, Delphine halted and turned. She smiled at Frank and called down to him.

"Live life to the full, my dear friend."

Then she turned around again, stepped forward, and disappeared into the white smoke.

Frank stood alone and forlorn in the snow. His tears were warm against his cold face.

They grabbed his arms and put them behind his back. He offered no resistance. There was a click as the handcuffs were locked into place around his wrists. But he didn't care about that. Frank's eyes were still fixed on the empty space where only a few moments ago Delphine had been standing.

CHAPTER 25

The air smelled of rosemary from the plants in their terracotta pots. On the other side of the old stone wall, gnarled olive trees stood, ancient sentinels in an ancient land.

In the gaps between them, the house roofs and church towers of Ragusa were visible. Although the setting sun, which appeared to rest on them, made it difficult to look in that direction for more than a second or two.

A crescendo of high-pitched buzzing from the cicadas made for a pleasing background noise to life here. Frank smiled with contentment, he'd found a home he never wanted to leave.

It had been a long journey through France and down the length of Italy. Brunhild only just made it. Frank would need to think about getting another car, but he wouldn't sell her. His faithful friend could live out her days here. A spare room should family or friends ever visit his small one bedroom, old stone cottage. Frank would sleep in Brunhild when he had guests and relive the journeys they'd made together.

"Have you gone completely mad, dad?" Dawn had said when he told her of his plans.

"You'll be home within six months. Mark my words," was Gayle's reaction. "You're too much of a stick in the mud, a creature of habit."

"I couldn't live there, they don't have proper beer like we do" and "Their football team's not bad, I grant you that. But what else do they have?" were two of the less negative reactions from the regulars at the Queen Mary pub when Frank revealed his intention to retire in Sicily.

Frank hadn't bothered arguing. After all, like them he used to have small horizons and be averse to change of any sort. He now knew that until you've had your eyes opened by experiencing something different, you won't ever believe anything other than what you already think, especially at his age.

Frank was sitting on the patio in a straight-backed wooden chair which he'd carried out from the house. It had come with the rest of the solid, antique furniture when he bought the property. He was holding a photo of Delphine which she had given him. He had taken it from his shirt pocket where he kept it, next to his heart. It was over a year but he still missed her and thought of her every day.

Observing a woman of a similar age to him coming up the dusty path between the trees, he put the photo back in its place.

"Buona sera."

"Buona sera," replied Frank standing up as she

opened the iron gate. "Sono inglese. Non parlo italiano."

He had taught himself a few basic phrases. Once unpacked, he would set about looking for a teacher. He'd read that learning a new language helped keep your brain younger.

"Well, you must learn how to speak Italian now that you come to live here. I speak some English but only a little. I came to ask you to dinner tonight. You must be tired after your long journey. We are neighbours, I live the other side of the field. The house with the green door."

"Thank you. That would be lovely."

"Good. Come for eight. I'll enjoy the company. It's quiet here since my husband died. Until later then. Ciao." She smiled at him before returning the way she'd come.

There was a warmth in her smile that reminded Frank of someone.

++++++++++++++++++++++++++++++++

ALSO BY DAVID CANFORD

The Shadows of Seville

A gripping and moving story of loss and love, of hatred and passion, and of horror and hope, set in Spain's most evocative city during the turmoil of the Spanish Civil War and the following decades. Lose yourself in vibrant 'Sevilla' where the shadows of the past are around every corner.

Puppets of Prague

Can the dream of freedom overcome fear and oppression? Friendships are tested to the limit in this saga spanning Prague's tumultuous 20th century. In the summer of 1914 young love beckons and the future seems bright for three close friends, but momentous events throw into stark relief the differences between them that had never mattered before.

Betrayal in Venice

Sent to Venice on a secret mission against the Nazis, a soldier finds his life unexpectedly altered when he saves a young woman at the end of World War Two. Discovering the truth many years later, Glen Butler's reaction to it betrays the one he loves most.

A Good Nazi? The Lies We Keep

Growing up in 1930s Germany two boys, one Catholic and one Jewish, become close friends. After Hitler seizes power, their lives are changed forever. When World War 2 comes, will they help each other, or will secrets from their teenage years make them enemies?

Kurt's War - The Boy who knew too much

Kurt is an English evacuee with a difference. His father is a Nazi. As Kurt grows into an adult and is forced to pretend that he is someone he isn't for his own protection, will he survive in the hostile world in which he must live? And with his enemies closing in, will even the woman he loves believe who he really is?

The Throwback - The Girl who wasn't wanted

A baby's birth on a South Carolina plantation threatens to cause a scandal, but the funeral of mother and child seems to ensure that the truth will never be known. A family saga of hatred, revenge, forbidden love, overcoming hardship and helping others.

Sweet Bitter Freedom

The sequel to the Throwback. Though the Civil War has now ended, Mosa is confronted by new challenges and old adversaries who are determined to try and take what she has. While some hope to build a new South, the old South refuses to die. Will Mosa lose everything or find a way through?

A Heart Left Behind

New Yorker, Orla, finds herself trapped in a web of secret love, blackmail and espionage in the build up to WW2. Moving to Berlin and hoping to escape her past, she is forced to undertake a task that will cost not only her own life but also that of her son if she fails.

Bound Bayou

A young teacher from England achieves a dream when he gets the chance to work for a year in the United States, but 1950s Mississippi is not the America he has seen on the movie screens at home. When his independent spirit collides with the rules of life in the Deep South, he sets off a chain of events he can't control.

Sea Snakes and Cannibals

A travelogue of visits to islands around the world, including remote Fijian islands, Corsica, islands in the Sea of Cortez, Mexico, and the Greek islands.

When the Water Runs Out

Will water shortage result in the USA invading Canada? One person can stop a war if he isn't killed first but is he a hero or a traitor? When two very different worlds collide, the outcome is on a knife-edge.

2045 The Last Resort

In 2045 those who lost their jobs to robots are taken care of in resorts where life is an endless vacation. For those still in work, the American dream has never been better. But is all quite as perfect as it seems?

THANK YOU

I hope you enjoyed reading 'Going Big or Small?'. I would appreciate it if you could spare a few moments to post a review on Amazon. It only need be a few words.

Thanks so much,

David Canford

ABOUT THE AUTHOR

Writing historical fiction, David Canford is able to combine his love of history and travel in novels that take readers on a rollercoaster journey through time and place with characters who face struggle and hardship but where resilience, love and forgiveness can overcome hatred and oppression.

He has also written two novels about the future, and a travelogue.

David has three grown up daughters and lives on the south coast of England with his wife and their dog.

You can contact him via his Facebook page or at David.Canford@hotmail.com

Printed in Great Britain
by Amazon